YOUNG
TÖRLES

ABOUT THE AUTHOR

Robert Musil was born in Austria in 1880. He attended military academy at Mahrisch-Weisskirchen in Moravia before studying engineering in Brno and experimental psychology in Berlin. Fleeing Berlin in the wake of the Nazi takeover, Musil left Vienna in 1938 for the same reason, settling in Geneva, where he died on April 15, 1942.

After spending the First World War on the Italian front, where he was an officer in the Austrian army, Musil served in the Austrian government until 1922, at which time he devoted himself exclusively to writing. His *A Man Without Qualities*, an immense work published in part after his death, is widely considered one of the most important works of twentieth-century literature. His first novel, *Young Törless*, was published in 1906 to immediate acclaim.

YOUNG TÖRLESS

Robert Musil

Translated from the German by
Eithne Wilkins and Ernst Kaiser

Pantheon Books
New York

Library of Congress Cataloging in Publication Data

Musil, Robert, 1880-1942.
   Young Törless.

   Translation of: Die Verwirrungen des Zöglings
Törless.
   Reprint. Originally published: New York:
Pantheon, 1955.
   I. Title.
PT2625.U8V413   1982   833'.912   81-19003
ISBN 0-394-71015-0   AACR2

" *In some strange way we devalue things as soon as we give utter-ance to them. We believe we have dived to the uttermost depths of the abyss, and yet when we return to the surface the drop of water on our pallid finger-tips no longer resembles the sea from which it came. We think we have discovered a hoard of wonderful treasure-trove, yet when we emerge again into the light of day we see that all we have brought back with us is false stones and chips of glass. But for all this, the treasure goes on glimmering in the darkness, unchanged.*"

MAETERLINCK

IT was a small station on the long railroad to Russia.
Four parallel lines of iron rails extended endlessly in
each direction on the yellow gravel of the broad track—
each fringed, as with a dirty shadow, with the dark strip
burnt into the ground by steam and fumes.

Behind the station, a low oil-painted building, there was
a broad, worn dirt-road leading up to the railway embank-
ment. It merged into the trampled ground, its edges indicated only by the two rows of acacia trees that flanked it
drearily, their thirsty leaves suffocated by dust and soot.

Perhaps it was these sad colours, or perhaps it was the
wan, exhausted light of the afternoon sun, drained of its
strength by the haze : there was something indifferent,
lifeless, and mechanical about objects and human beings
here, as though they were all part of a scene in a puppet-
theatre. From time to time, at regular intervals, the
station-master stepped out of his office and, always with
the same turn of his head, glanced up the long line towards
the signal-box, where the signals still failed to indicate
the approach of the express each time, which had been
delayed for a long time at the frontier ; then, always with
the very same movement of his arm, he would pull out
his pocket-watch and, then, shaking his head, he would
disappear again: just so do the figures on ancient tower-
clocks appear and disappear again with the striking of
the hour.

On the broad, well-trodden strip of ground between
the railway-line and the station building a gay company

of young men was strolling up and down, walking to right and to left of a middle-aged couple who were the centre of the somewhat noisy conversation. But even the blitheness of this group did not ring quite true; it was as if their merry laughter fell into silence only a few paces away, almost as if it had run into some invisible but solid obstacle and there sunk to the ground.

Frau Hofrat Törless—this was the lady, perhaps forty years of age—wore a thick veil concealing her sad eyes, which were a little reddened from weeping. This was a leave-taking. And she found it hard, yet once again, having to leave her only child among strangers for so long a period, without any chance to watch protectively over her darling.

For the little town lay far away from the capital, in the eastern territories of the empire, in thinly populated, dry arable country.

The reason why Frau Törless had to leave her boy in this remote and inhospitable outlandish district was that in this town there was a celebrated boarding-school, which in the previous century had developed out of a religious foundation and had since remained where it was, doubtless in order to safeguard the young generation, in its years of awakening, from the corrupting influences of a large city.

It was here that the sons of the best families in the country received their education, going on then to the university, or into the army or the service of the State; in all such careers, as well as for general social reasons, it was a particular advantage to have been educated at W.

Four years previously this consideration had caused Hofrat and Frau Törless to yield to their son's ambitious plea and arrange for him to enter this school.

This decision afterwards cost many tears. For almost from the first moment when the doors of the school closed behind him with irrevocable finality, little Törless suffered from frightful, agonising homesickness. Neither lessons, nor games on the wide luxuriant grasslands of the park, nor the other distractions that the school offered its inmates, could hold his attention ; he took almost no interest in these things. He saw everything only as through a veil and even during the day often had trouble in gulping down an obstinately rising sob ; at night he always cried himself to sleep.

He wrote letters home almost daily, and he lived only in these letters ; everything else he did seemed to him only a shadowy, unmeaning string of events, indifferent stations on his way, like the marking of the hours on a clock-face. But when he wrote he felt within himself something that made him distinct, that set him apart ; something in him rose, like an island of miraculous suns and flashing colours, out of the ocean of grey sensations that lapped around him, cold and indifferent, day after day. And when by day, at games or in class, he remembered that he would write his letter in the evening, it was as though he were wearing, hidden on his person, fastened to an invisible chain, a golden key with which, as soon as no one was looking, he would open the gate leading into marvellous gardens.

The remarkable thing about it was that this sudden consuming fondness for his parents was for himself something new and disconcerting. He had never imagined such a thing before, he had gone to boarding-school gladly and of his own free will, indeed he had laughed when at their first leave-taking his mother had been unable to check her tears ; and only later, when he had been on his own for some days and been getting on comparatively well, did it gush up in him suddenly and with elemental force.

He took it for homesickness and believed he was

missing his parents. But it was in reality something much more indefinable and complex. For the object of this longing, the image of his parents, actually ceased to have any place in it at all : I mean that certain plastic, physical memory of a loved person which is not merely remembrance but something speaking to all the senses and preserved in all the senses, so that one cannot do anything without feeling the other person silent and invisible at one's side. This soon faded out, like a resonance that vibrates only for a while. In other words, by that time Törless could no longer conjure up before his eyes the image of his 'dear, dear parents'—as he usually called them in his thoughts. If he tried to do so, what rose up in its place was the boundless grief and longing from which he suffered so much and which yet held him in its spell, its hot flames causing him both agony and rapture. And so the thought of his parents more and more became a mere pretext, an external means to set going this egoistic suffering in him, which enclosed him in his voluptuous pride as in the seclusion of a chapel where, surrounded by hundreds of flickering candles and hundreds of eyes gazing down from sacred images, incense was wafted among the writhing flagellants. . . .

Later, as his ' homesickness ' became less violent and gradually passed off, this, its real character, began to show rather more clearly. For in its place there did not come the contentment that might have been expected ; on the contrary, what it left in young Törless's soul was a void. And this nothingness, this emptiness in himself, made him realise that it was no mere yearning he had lost, but something positive, a spiritual force, something that had flowered in him under the guise of grief.

But now it was all over, and this well-spring of a first sublime bliss had made itself known to him only by its drying up.

4

At this time the passionate evidence of the soul's awakening vanished out of his letters, and in its place came detailed descriptions of life at school and the new friends he had made.

He himself felt impoverished by this change, and bare, like a little tree experiencing its first winter after its first still fruitless blossoming.

But his parents were glad. They loved him with strong, unthinking, animal affection. Every time after he had been home on holiday from boarding-school, and gone away again, to the Frau Hofrat the house once more seemed empty and deserted, and for some days after each of these visits it was with tears in her eyes that she went through the rooms, here and there caressing some object on which the boy's gaze had rested or which his fingers had held. And both parents would have let themselves be torn to pieces for his sake.

The clumsy pathos and passionate, mutinous sorrow of his letters had given them grievous concern and kept them in a state of high-pitched sensitiveness; the blithe, contented light-heartedness that followed upon it gladdened them again and, feeling that now a crisis had been surmounted, they did all they could to encourage this new mood.

Neither in the one phase nor in the other did they recognise the symptoms of a definite psychological development; on the contrary, they accepted both the anguish and its appeasement as merely a natural consequence of the situation. It escaped them that a young human being, all on his own, had made his first, unsuccessful attempt to develop the forces of his inner life.

* * *

Törless, however, now felt very dissatisfied and groped

this way and that, in vain, for something new that might serve as a support to him.

* * *

At this period there was an episode symptomatic of something still germinating in Törless, which was to develop significantly in him later.

What happened was this : one day the youthful Prince H. entered the school, a scion of one of the oldest, most influential, and most conservative noble families in the empire.

All the others thought him boring, and found his gentle gaze affected ; the manner in which he stood with one hip jutting forward and, while talking, languidly interlocked and unlocked his fingers, they mocked as effeminate. But what chiefly aroused their scorn was that he had been brought to the school not by his parents but by his former tutor, a doctor of divinity who was a member of a religious order.

On Törless, however, he made a strong impression from the very first moment. Perhaps the fact that he was a prince and by birth entitled to move in Court circles had something to do with it ; but however that might be, he was a different kind of person for Törless to get to know.

The silence and tranquillity of an ancient and noble country seat, and of devotional exercises, seemed somehow to cling about him still. When he walked, it was with smooth, lithe movements and with that faintly diffident attitude of withdrawal, that contraction of the body, which comes from being accustomed to walking very erect through a succession of vast, empty rooms, where any other sort of person seems to bump heavily against invisible corners of the empty space around him.

And so for Törless acquaintance with the prince became

6

a source of exquisite psychological enjoyment. It laid
the foundations in him of that kind of knowledge of
human nature which teaches one to recognise and appreciate another person by the cadence of his voice, by
the way he picks up and handles a thing, even, indeed,
by the timbre of his silences and the expressiveness of
his bodily attitude in adjusting himself to a space, a
setting—in other words, by that mobile, scarcely tangible,
and yet essential, integral way of being a human entity,
a spirit, that way of being it which encloses the core,
the palpable and debatable aspect of him, as flesh encloses the mere bones—and in so appreciating to pre-
figure for oneself the mental aspect of his personality.

During this brief period Törless lived as in an idyll.
He was not put out by his new friend's devoutness,
which was really something quite alien to him, coming
as he did from a free-thinking middle-class family. He
accepted it without a qualm, going so far as to see it,
indeed, as something especially admirable in the prince,
since it intensified the essential quality of this other boy's
personality, which he felt was so unlike his own as to
be in no way comparable.

In the prince's company he felt rather as though he
were in some little chapel far off the main road. The
thought of actually not belonging there quite vanished
the enjoyment of, for once, seeing the daylight through
glass ; and he let his gaze glide over the profusion
agalma in this other person's soul until
at least some sort of indistinct picture
as though with his finger-tips he were
es of an arabesque, not thinking about it,
ng the beautiful pattern of it, which twined
to some weird laws beyond his ken.
then suddenly there came the break between

Törless blundered badly, as he had to admit to himself afterwards.

The fact was : on one occasion they did suddenly find themselves arguing about religion. And as soon as that happened, it was really all over and done with. For as though independently of himself, Törless's intellect lashed out, inexorably, at the sensitive young prince ; he poured out torrents of a rationalist's scorn upon him, barbarously desecrating the filigree habitation in which the other boy's soul dwelt. And they parted in anger.

After that they never spoke to each other again. Törless was indeed obscurely aware that what he had done was senseless, and a glimmer of intuitive insight told him that his wooden yardstick of rationality had untimely shattered a relationship that was subtle and full of rare fascination. But this was something he simply had not been able to help. It left him, probably for ever, with a sort of yearning for what had been ; yet he seemed to have been caught up in another current, which was carrying him further and further away in a different direction.

And then some time later the prince, who had not been happy there, left the school.

* * *

Now everything around Törless was empty and boring. But meanwhile he had been growing older, and with the onset of adolescence something began to rise up in him, darkly and steadily. At this stage of his development he made some new friends, of a kind corresponding to the needs of his age, which were to be of very great importance to him. He became friends with Beineberg and Reiting, and with Moté and Hofmeier, the boys in whose company he was today seeing his parents off at the railway station.

8

Remarkably enough, these were the boys who counted as the worst of his year; they were gifted and, it went without saying, of good family, but at times they were wild and reckless to the point of brutality. And that it should be precisely their company to which Törless now felt so strongly drawn was doubtless connected with his own lack of self-certainty, which had become very marked indeed since he had lost touch with the prince. It was indeed the logical continuation of that break, for, like the break itself, it indicated some fear of all over-subtle toyings with emotions; and by contrast with that sort of thing the nature of these other friends stood out as sound and sturdy, giving life its due.

Törless entirely abandoned himself to their influence, for the situation in which his mind now found itself was approximately this . . . At schools of the kind known as the *Gymnasium*, at his age, one has read Goethe, Schiller, Shakespeare, and perhaps even some modern writers too, and this, having been half digested, is then written out of the system again, excreted, as it were, through the finger-tips. Roman tragedies are written, or poems, of the most sensitive lyrical kind, that go through their paces garbed in punctuation that is looped over whole pages at a time, as in delicate lace: things that are in themselves ludicrous, but which are of inestimable value in contributing to a sound development. For these associations originating outside, and these borrowed emotions, carry young people over the dangerously soft spiritual ground of the years in which they need to be of some significance to themselves and nevertheless are still too incomplete to have any real significance. Whether any residue of it is ultimately left in the one, or nothing in the other, does not matter; later each will somehow come to terms with himself, and the danger exists only in the stage of transition. If at that period

9

one could bring a boy to see the ridiculousness of himself, the ground would give way under him, or he would plunge headlong like a somnambulist who, suddenly awaking, sees nothing but emptiness around him.

That illusion, that conjuring trick for the benefit of the personality's development, was missing in this school. For though the classics were there in the library, they were considered ' boring ', and for the rest there were only volumes of sentimental romances and drearily humorous tales of army life.

Young Törless had read just about all of them in his sheer greed for books, and this or that conventionally tender image from one story or another did sometimes linger for a while in his mind ; but none had any influence —any real influence—on his character.

At this period it seemed that he had no character at all.

Under the influence of this reading, he himself now and then would write a little story or begin an epic romance, and in his excitement over the sufferings of his heroes, crossed in love, his cheeks would flush, his pulse quicken, and his eyes shine.

But when he laid down his pen, it was all over ; his spirit lived only, as it were, while in motion. And so too he found it possible to dash off a poem or a story at any time, whenever it might be required of him. The doing of it excited him, yet he never took it quite seriously, and this occupation in itself did not strike him as important. Nothing of it was assimilated into his personality, nor did it originate within his personality. All that happened was that under some external pressure he underwent emotions that transcended the indifference of ordinary life, just as an actor needs the compulsion that a role imposes on him.

These were cerebral reactions. But what is felt to be character or soul, a person's inner contour or aura, that is to say, the thing in contrast with which the thoughts, decisions, and actions appear random, lacking in characteristic quality, and easily exchangeable for others—the thing that had, for instance, bound Törless to the prince in a manner beyond the reach of any intellectual judgment —this ultimate, immovable background seemed to be utterly lost to Törless at this period.

In his friends it was enjoyment of sport, the animal delight in being alive, that prevented them from feeling the need for anything of this kind, just as at the *Gymnasium* the want is supplied by the sport with literature.

But Törless's constitution was too intellectual for the one, and, as for the other, life at this school, where one had to be in a perpetual state of readiness to settle arguments with one's fists, made him keenly sensitive to the absurdity of such borrowed sentiment. So his being took on a vagueness, a sort of inner helplessness, that made it impossible for him to be sure where he stood.

He attached himself to these new friends because he was impressed by their wildness. Since he was ambitious, he now and then even tried to outvie them in this. But each time he would leave off half-way, and on this account had to put up with no small amount of gibes, which would scare him back into himself again. At this critical period the whole of his life really consisted in nothing but these efforts, renewed again and again, to emulate his rough, more masculine friends and, counterbalancing that, a deep inner indifference to all such strivings.

Now, when his parents came to see him, so long as they were alone he was quiet and shy. Each time he dodged his mother's affectionate caresses under one pretext or another He would really have liked to yield to them, but he was ashamed, as though he were being watched by his friends.

11

His parents let it pass as the awkwardness of adolescence.

Then in the afternoon the whole noisy crowd would come along. They played cards, ate, drank, told anecdotes about the masters, and smoked the cigarettes that the Hofrat had brought from the capital.

This jollity pleased and reassured the parents.

That there were, in between times, hours of a different kind for Törless was something they did not know. And recently there had been more and more of such hours. There were moments when life at school became a matter of utter indifference to him. Then the putty of his everyday concerns dropped out and, with nothing more to bind them together, the hours of his life fell apart.

He often sat for a long time—gloomily brooding—as it were hunched over himself.

*   *   *

This time too his parents had stayed for two days. There had been a lunching and dining together, smoking, a drive in the country ; and now the express was to carry Törless's parents back to the capital.

A faint vibration of the rails heralded the train's approach, and the bell clanging on the station roof sounded inexorably in the Frau Hofrat's ears.

" Well, my dear Beineberg, so you'll keep an eye on this lad of mine for me, won't you ? " Hofrat Törless said, turning to young Baron Beineberg, a lanky, bony boy with big ears that stuck out, and eyes that were expressive and intelligent.

Törless, who was younger and smaller than the others, pulled a face at this repugnant suggestion of being given into his friend's charge ; and Beineberg grinned, obviously flattered and with a shade of triumphant malice.

" Really," the Hofrat added, turning to the rest of

them, " I should like to ask you all, if there should be anything at all the matter with my son, to let me know at once."

This was going too far, and it drew from young Törless an infinitely wearied protest : " But, Father, what on earth do you think could happen to me ? " although he was well used by now to having to put up with this excess of solicitude at every leave-taking.

Meanwhile the others drew themselves up, clicking their heels, each straightening the elegant sword at his side. And the Hofrat went on : " One never knows what may happen. It is a great weight off my mind to know I would be instantly informed. After all, something might prevent you from writing."

At that moment the train drew in. Hofrat Törless embraced his son, Frau von Törless drew the veil tighter over her face to hide her tears, and one after the other the friends once more expressed their thanks for having been entertained. Then the guard slammed the door of the carriage.

Once again Hofrat and Frau von Törless saw the high, bare back of the school building and the immense, long wall surrounding the park; and then there was nothing to left and to right but grey-brown fields and an occasional fruit-tree.

* * *

Meanwhile the boys had left the railway station and were walking, in two single files, along the two edges of the road—so avoiding at least the densest and most suffocating dust—towards the town, without talking to each other much.

It was after five o'clock, and over the fields came a breath of something solemn and cold, a harbinger of evening.

13

Törless began to feel very mournful.

Perhaps it was because of his parents' departure, or perhaps it was caused only by the forbidding stolid melancholy that now lay like a dead weight on all the landscape, blurring the outlines of things, even a few paces away, with lack-lustre heaviness.

The same dreadful indifference that had been blanketed over the surrounding countryside all that afternoon now came creeping across the plain, and after it, like a slimy trail, came the mist, stickily clinging to the fresh-ploughed fields and the leaden-grey acres of turnips. Törless did not glance to right or to left, but he felt it. Steadily as he walked he set his feet in the tracks gaping in the dust, the prints left by the footsteps of the boy in front—and he felt it as though it must be so, as a stony compulsion catching his whole life up and compressing it into this movement—steadily plodding on along this one line, along this one small streak being drawn out through the dust.

When they came to a halt at a crossroads, where a second road and their own road debouched into a round, worn patch of ground, and where a rotten timber sign-post pointed crookedly into the air, the tilted line of it, in such contrast with the surroundings, struck Törless as being like a cry of desperation.

Again they walked on. Törless thought of his parents, of people he knew, of life. At this time of day people were changing for a party or deciding they would go to the theatre. And afterwards one might go to a restaurant, hear a band playing, sit at a café table. . . . One met interesting people. A flirtation, an adventure, kept one in suspense till the morning. Life went on revolving, churning out ever new and unexpected happenings, like a strange and wonderful wheel. . . .

Törless sighed over these thoughts, and at each step

that bore him closer to the cramped narrowness of school something in him constricted, a noose was pulled tighter and tighter.

Even now the bell was ringing in his ears. And there was nothing he dreaded so much as this ringing of the bell, which cut the day short, once and for all, like the savage slash of a knife.

To be sure, there was nothing for him to experience, and his life passed along in a blur of perpetual indifference ; but this ringing of the bell was an added mockery, which left him quivering with helpless rage against himself, his fate, and the day that was buried.

Now you can't experience anything more at all, for twelve hours you can't experience anything, for twelve hours you're dead. . . . That was what this bell meant.

*　　*　　*

When the little band of friends reached the first low-built wretched cottages, this mood of gloom and introspection lifted from Törless. As though seized by some sudden interest, he raised his head and glanced intently into the smoky interior of the dirty little hovels they were passing.

Outside the doors of most of them the women-folk were standing, in their wide skirts and coarse shifts, their broad feet caked with dust, their arms bare and brown.

If they were young and buxom, some crude Slav jest would be flung at them. They would nudge each other and titter at ‘ the young gentlemen ’ ; sometimes, too, one would utter a shriek when her breasts were too vigorously brushed against in passing, or would answer a slap on the buttocks with an insulting epithet and a burst of laughter. There were others who merely watched the swift passers-by with a grave and angry look ;

15

and the peasant himself, if he happened to have come on the scene, would smile awkwardly, half unsure what to make of it, half in good humour.

Törless took no part in this display of overweening and precocious manliness.

The reason for this lay doubtless to some extent in a certain timidity about sexual matters such as is characteristic of almost all only children, but chiefly in his own peculiar kind of sensuality, which was more deeply hidden, more forceful, and of a darker hue than that of his friends and more slow and difficult in its manifestations.

While the others were making a show of shameless behaviour with the women, rather more for the sake of being ' smart ' than from any lascivious urge, the taciturn little Törless's soul was in a state of upheaval, surging with real shamelessness.

He looked through the little windows and the crooked, narrow doorways into the interior of the cottages with a gaze burning so hotly that there was all the time something like a delicate mesh dancing before his eyes.

Almost naked children tumbled about in the mud of the yards ; here and there as some woman bent over her work her skirt swung high, revealing the hollows at the back of her knees, or the bulge of a heavy breast showed as the linen tightened over it. It was as though all this were going on in some quite different, animal, oppressive atmosphere, and the cottages exuded a heavy, sluggish air, which Törless eagerly breathed in.

He thought of old paintings that he had seen in museums without really understanding them. He was waiting for something, just as, when he stood in front of those paintings, he had always been waiting for something that never happened. What was it. . . ? It must be something surprising, something never beheld before, some monstrous sight of which he could not form the slightest notion; something of a terrifying, beast-like sensuality; something that would seize him in its claws and rend him, starting with his eyes; an experience that in some still utterly obscure way seemed to be associated with these women's soiled petticoats, with their roughened hands, with the low ceilings of their little rooms, with . . . with a besmirching of himself with the filth of these yards . . . No, no . . . Now he no longer felt anything but the fiery net before his eyes; the words did not say it; for it is not nearly so bad as the words make it seem; it is something mute—a choking in the throat, a scarcely perceptible thought, and only if one insisted on getting it to the point of words would it come out like that. And then it has ceased to be anything but faintly reminiscent of whatever it was, as under huge magnification, when one not only sees everything more distinctly but also sees things that are not there at all. . . . And yet, for all that, it was something to be ashamed of.

*   *   *

" Is Baby feeling homesick ? " he was suddenly asked, in mocking tones, by von Reiting, that tall boy two years older than himself, who had been struck by Törless's silence and the darkness over his eyes. Törless forced an artificial and rather embarrassed smile to his lips; and he felt as though the malicious Reiting had been eavesdropping on what had been going on within him.

He did not answer. But meanwhile they had reached the little town's church square, with its cobbles, and here they parted company.

Törless and Beineberg did not want to go back yet, but the others had no leave to stay out any longer and returned to the school.

THE two boys had gone along to the cake shop.

Here they sat at a little round table, beside a window overlooking the garden, under a gas candelabrum with its flames buzzing softly in the milky glass globes.

They had made themselves thoroughly comfortable, having little glasses filled up now with this liqueur, now with another, smoking cigarettes, and eating pastries between whiles, enjoying the luxury of being the only customers. Although in one of the back rooms there might still be some solitary visitor sitting over his glass of wine, at least here in front all was quiet, and even the portly, ageing proprietress seemed to have dozed off behind the counter.

Törless gazed—but vaguely—through the window, out into the empty garden, where darkness was slowly gathering.

Beineberg was talking—about India, as usual. For his father, the general, had as a young officer been there in British service. And he had brought back not only what any other European brought back with him, carvings, textiles, and little idols manufactured for sale to tourists, but something of a feeling, which he had never lost, for the mysterious, bizarre glimmerings of esoteric Buddhism. Whatever he had picked up there, and had come to know more of from his later reading, he had passed on to his son, even from the boy's early childhood.

For the rest, his attitude to reading was an odd one. He was a cavalry officer and was not at all fond of books in general. Novels and philosophy he despised equally. When he read, he did not want to reflect on opinions and controversies but, from the very instant of opening the book, to enter as through a secret portal into the midst of some very exclusive knowledge. Books that he read had to be such that the mere possession of them was as it were a secret sign of initiation and a pledge of more than earthly revelations. And this he found only in books of Indian philosophy, which to him seemed to be not merely books, but revelations, something real—keys snch as were the alchemical and magical books of the Middle Ages.

With them this healthy, energetic man, who observed his duties strictly and exercised his three horses himself almost every day, would usually shut himself up for the evening.

Then he would pick out a passage at random and meditate on it, in the hope that this time it would reveal its inmost secret meaning to him. Nor was he ever disappointed, however often he had to admit that he had not yet advanced beyond the forecourts of the sacred temple.

Thus it was that round this sinewy, tanned, open-air man there hovered something like the nimbus of an esoteric mystery. His conviction of being daily on the eve of receiving some overpoweringly great illumination gave him an air of reserve and superiority. His eyes were not dreamy, but calm and hard. The habit of reading books in which no single word could be shifted from its place without disturbing the secret significance, the careful, scrupulous weighing of every single sentence for its meaning and counter-meaning, its possible ambiguities, had brought that look into those eyes.

Only occasionally did his thoughts lose themselves in a twilit state of agreeable melancholy. This happened when he thought of the esoteric cult bound up with the originals of the writings open before him, of the miracles that had emanated from them, stirring thousands, thousands of human beings who now, because of the vast distance separating him from them, appeared to him like brothers, while he despised the people round about him, whom he saw in all their detail. At such hours he grew despondent. He was depressed by the thought that he was condemned to spend his life far away from the sources of those holy powers and that his efforts were perhaps doomed in the end to be frustrated by these unfavourable conditions. But then, after he had been sitting gloomily over his books for a while, he would begin to have a strange feeling. True, his melancholy lost nothing of its oppressiveness—on the contrary, the sadness of it was still further intensified—but it no longer oppressed him. He would then feel more forlorn than ever, and as though defending a lost position; but in this mournfulness there lay a subtle relish, a pride in doing something utterly alien to the people about him, serving a divinity uncomprehended by the rest. And then it was that, fleetingly, something would flare up in his eyes that was like the ravishment of religious ecstasy.

*   *   *

Beineberg had talked himself to a standstill. In him the image of his eccentric father lived on in a kind of distorted magnification. Every feature was preserved; but what in the other had originally, perhaps, been no more than a mood that was conserved and intensified for the sake of its exclusiveness had in him grown hugely into a fantastic hope. That peculiarity of his father's, which for the older man was at bottom perhaps really no more than that last refuge for individuality which every human being—and even if it is only through his choice of clothes—must provide himself with in order to have something to distinguish him from others, had in him turned into the firm belief that he could achieve dominion over people by means of more than ordinary spiritual powers.

Törless knew this talk by heart. It passed away over him, leaving him almost quite unmoved.

He had now turned slightly from the window and was observing Beineberg, who was rolling himself a cigarette. And again he felt the queer repugnance, the dislike of Beineberg, that would at times rise up in him. These slim, dark hands, which were now so deftly rolling the tobacco into the paper, were really—come to think of it—beautiful. Thin fingers, oval, beautifully curved nails : there was a touch of breeding, of elegance, about them. So there was too in the dark brown eyes. It was there also in the long-drawn lankiness of the whole body. To be sure, the ears did stick out more than would quite do, the face was small and irregular, and the sum total of the head's expression was reminiscent of a bat's. Nevertheless—Törless felt this quite clearly as he weighed the details against each other in the balance —it was not the ugly, it was precisely the more attractive features that made him so peculiarly uneasy.

The thinness of the body—Beineberg himself was in the habit of lauding the steely, slender legs of Homeric champion runners as the ideal—did not at all have this effect on him. Törless had never yet tried to give himself an account of this, and for the moment he could not think of any satisfactory comparison. He would have liked to scrutinise Beineberg more closely, but then Beineberg would have noticed what he was thinking and he would have had to strike up some sort of conversation. Yet it was precisely thus—half looking at him, half filling the picture out in his imagination—that he was struck by the difference. If he thought the clothes away from the body, it became quite impossible to hold on to the notion of calm slenderness; what happened then, instantly, was that in his mind's eye he saw restless, writhing movements, a twisting of limbs and a bending of the spine such as are to be found in all pictures of martyrs' deaths, or in the grotesque performances of acrobats and ' rubber men ' at fairs.

And the hands, too, which he could certainly just as well have pictured in some beautifully expressive gesture, he could not imagine otherwise than in motion, with flickering fingers. And it was precisely on these hands, which were really Beineberg's most attractive feature, that his greatest repugnance was concentrated. There was something prurient about them. That no doubt, was, what it amounted to. And there was for him something prurient, too, about the body, which he could not help associating with dislocated movements. But it was in the hands that this seemed to accumulate, and it seemed to radiate from them like a hint of some touch that was yet to come, sending a thrill of disgust coursing over Törless's skin. He himself was astonished at the notion, and faintly shocked. For this was now the second time today that something sexual had without warning, and irrelevantly, thrust its way in among his thoughts.

Beineberg had taken up a newspaper, and now Törless could consider him closely.

There was in reality scarcely anything to be found in his appearance that could have even remotely justified this sudden association of ideas in Törless's mind.

And for all that, in spite of the lack of justification for it, his sense of discomfort grew ever more intense. The silence between them had lasted scarcely ten minutes, and yet Törless felt his repugnance gradually increasing to the utmost degree. A fundamental mood, a fundamental relationship between himself and Beineberg, seemed in this way to be manifesting itself for the first time; a mistrust that had always been lurking somewhere in the depths seemed all at once to have loomed up into the realm of conscious feeling.

The atmosphere became more and more acutely uncomfortable. Törless was invaded by an urge to utter insults, but he could find no adequate words. He was uneasy with a sort of shame, as though something had actually happened between himself and Beineberg. His fingers began to drum restlessly on the table.

*　　*　　*

Finally, in order to escape from this strange state of mind, he looked out of the window again.

Now Beineberg glanced up from the newspaper. Then he read a paragraph aloud, laid the paper aside, and yawned.

With the breaking of the silence the spell that had bound Törless was also broken. Casual words began to flow over the awkward moment, blotting it out. There had been a momentary alertness, but now the old indifference was there again. . . .

" How long have we still got ? " Törless asked.

" Two and a half hours."

Suddenly shivering, Törless hunched up his shoulders. Once again he felt the paralysing weight of the constriction he was about to re-enter, the school time-table, the daily companionship of his friends. Even that dislike of Beineberg would cease which seemed, for an instant, to have created a new situation.

" . . . What's for supper tonight ? "

" I don't know."

" What have we got tomorrow ? "

" Mathematics."

" Oh. Was there something to prepare ? "

" Yes. A few new trigonometry theorems. But you needn't worry about them, they're not difficult."

" And what else ? "

" Divinity."

" Divinity. . . . Oh, well. That's something to look forward to. . . . I think when I really get going I could just as easily prove that twice two is five as that there can be only one God. . . ."

Beineberg glanced up at Törless mockingly. " It's quite funny how you go on about that. It strikes me almost as if you really enjoyed it. Anyway, there's a positive glare of enthusiasm in your eyes. . . ."

" And why not ? Don't you think it's fun ? There's always a point you get to where you stop knowing whether you're just making it all up or if what you've made up is truer than you are yourself."

" How do you mean ? "

" Well, I don't mean literally, of course. Naturally, you always know you *are* making it up. But all the same, every now and then the whole thing strikes you as being so credible that you're brought up standing, in a way, in the grip of your own ideas."

" Well, but what is it about it you enjoy, then ? "

" Just that : you get a sort of jerk in your head, a sort of dizziness, a shock . . ."

" Oh, I say, shut up ! That's all foolery."

" Well, I didn't say it wasn't. But still, so far as I'm concerned it's more interesting than anything else at school."

" It's just a way of doing gymnastics with your brain. But it doesn't get you anywhere, all the same."

" No," Törless said, looking out into the garden again. Behind his back—as though from a long way off—he heard the buzzing of the gas-lights. He was preoccupied

24

by an emotion rising up in him, mournfully and like a mist.

"It doesn't get you anywhere. You're right about that. But it doesn't do to tell yourself that. How much of all the things we spend our whole time in school doing is really going to get anyone anywhere? What do we get anything out of? I mean for ourselves— you see what I mean? In the evening you know you've lived another day, you've learnt this and that, you've kept up with the time-table, but still, you're empty— inwardly, I mean. Right inside, you're still hungry, so to speak . . ."

Beineberg muttered something about exercising the mind by way of preparation—not yet being able to start on anything—later on . . .

"Preparation? Exercise? What *for*? Have you got any definite idea of it? I dare say you're hoping for something, but it's just as vague to you as it is to me. It's like this : everlastingly waiting for something you don't know anything about except that you're waiting for it. . . . It's so boring. . . ."

"Boring . . ." Beineberg drawled in mimicry, wagging his head.

Törless was still gazing out into the garden. He thought he could hear the rustling of the withered leaves being blown into drifts by the wind. Then came that moment of utter stillness which always occurs a little while before the descent of complete darkness. The shapes of things, which had been sinking ever more deeply into the dusk, and the blurring, dissolving colours of things—for an instant it all seemed to pause, to hover, as it were with a holding of the breath . . .

"You know, Beineberg," Törless said, without turning round, "when it's getting dark there always seem to be a few moments that are sort of different. Every time I watch it happening I remember the same thing : once when I was quite small I was playing in the woods at this time of evening. My nursemaid had wandered off somewhere. I didn't know she had, and so I still felt as if she were nearby. Suddenly something made me look up. I could feel I was alone. It was suddenly all so quiet. And when I looked around it was as though the trees were standing in a circle round me, all silent, and looking at me. I began to cry. I felt the grown-ups had deserted me and abandoned me to inanimate beings. . . . What is it ? I still often get it. What's this sudden silence that's like a language we can't hear ? "

"I don't know the thing you mean. But why shouldn't things have a language of their own ? After all, there are no definite grounds for asserting that they haven't a soul ! "

Törless did not answer. He did not care for Beineberg's speculative view of the matter.

But after a while Beineberg went on : " Why do you keep on staring out of the window ? What is there to be seen ? "

"I'm still wondering what it can be." But actually he had gone on to thinking about something else, which he did not want to speak of. That high tension, that harkening as if some solemn mystery might become audible, and the burden of gazing right into the midst of the still undefined relationships of things—all this was something he had been able to endure only for a moment. Then he had once again been overcome by the sense of solitude and forlornness which always followed this excessive demand upon his resources. He felt : there's something in this that's still too difficult for me. And his thoughts took refuge in something else, which was also implicit in it all, but which, as it were, lay only in the background and biding its time : loneliness.

26

From the deserted garden a leaf now and then fluttered up against the lit window, tearing a streak of brightness into the darkness behind it. Then the darkness seemed to shrink and withdraw, only in the next instant to advance again and stand motionless as a wall outside the window. This darkness was a world apart. It had descended upon the earth like a horde of black enemies, slaughtering or banishing human beings, or, whatever it did, blotting out all trace of them.

And it seemed to Törless that he was glad of this. At this moment he had no liking for human beings—for all who were adults. He never liked them when it was dark. He was in the habit then of cancelling them out of his thoughts. After that the world seemed to him like a sombre, empty house, and in his breast there was a sense of awe and horror, as though he must now search room after room—dark rooms where he did not know what the corners might conceal—groping his way across thresholds that no human foot would ever step on again, until—until in one room the doors would suddenly slam behind him and before him and he would stand confronting the mistress of the black hordes herself. And at the same instant the locks would snap shut in all the doors through which he had come; and only far beyond, outside the walls, would the shades of darkness stand on guard like black eunuchs, warding off any human approach.

This was his kind of loneliness since he had been left in the lurch that time—in the woods, where he had wept so bitterly. It held for him the lure of woman and of something monstrous. He felt it as a woman, but its breath was only a gasping in his chest, its face a whirling forgetfulness of all human faces, and the movements of its hands a shuddering all through his body. . . .

He feared this fantasy, for he was aware of the perverted

27

lust in the secrecy of it, and he was disturbed by the thought that such imaginings might gain more and more power over him. But they would overwhelm him just when he believed himself to be most serious and most pure. It happened, perhaps, as a reaction to those moments when he had an inkling of another emotional awareness, which, though it was already implicit in him, was as yet beyond his years. For there is, in the development of every fine moral energy, such an early point where it weakens the soul whose most daring experience it will perhaps be some day—just as if it had first to send down its roots, gropingly, to disturb the ground that they will afterwards hold together; and it is for this reason that boys with a great future ahead of them usually go through a period abounding in humiliations.

Törless's taste for certain moods was the first hint of a psychological development that was later to manifest itself as a strong sense of wonder. The fact was that later he was to have—and indeed to be dominated by—a peculiar ability : he could not help frequently experiencing events, people, things, and even himself, in such a way as to feel that in it all there was at once some insoluble enigma and some inexplicable kinship for which he could never quite produce any evidence. Then these things would seem tangibly comprehensible, and yet he could never entirely resolve them into words and ideas. Between events and himself, indeed between his own feelings and some inmost self that craved understanding of them, there always remained a dividing-line, which receded before his desire, like a horizon, the closer he tried to come to it. Indeed, the more accurately he circumscribed his feelings with thoughts, and the more familiar they became to him, the stranger and more incomprehensible did they seem to become, in equal measure; so that it no longer even seemed as though they were retreating before him, but as though he himself were withdrawing from them, and yet without being able to shake off the illusion of coming closer to them.

This queer antithesis, which was so difficult for him to grasp, later occupied an important phase of his spiritual development; it was something that tore at his soul, as though to rend it apart, and for a long time it was his soul's chief problem and the chief threat to it.

For the present, however, the severity of these struggles was indicated only by a frequent sudden lassitude, alarming him, as it were, from a long way off, when ever some ambiguous, odd mood—such as this just now—brought him a foreboding of it. Then he would seem to himself as powerless as a captive, as one who had been abandoned and shut away as much from himself as from others. At such times he could have screamed with desperation and the horror of emptiness; but instead of doing anything of the kind he would avert himself from this solemn and expectant, tormented, wearied being within himself and—still aghast at his abrupt renunciation—would begin to listen, more and more enchanted by their warm, sinful breath, to the whispering voices of his solitude.

*   *   *

Törless suddenly proposed that they should pay and go. A look of understanding gleamed in Beineberg's eyes: he knew and shared the mood. Törless was revolted by this concord, and his dislike of Beineberg quickened again; he felt himself degraded by their having anything in common.

But that had by now practically become part of it all.

Degradation is but one solitude more and yet another dark wall.

And so, without speaking to each other, they set out on a certain road.

THERE must have been a light shower of rain a few minutes earlier—the air was moist and heavy, a misty halo trembled round the street-lamps, and here and there the pavement glimmered.

Törless's sword clattered on the stones, and he drew it closer to his side. But there was still the sound of his heels on the pavement, and even that sent a queer shiver through him.

After a while, leaving the pavements of the town behind them, they had soft ground underfoot and were walking along wide village streets towards the river.

The water rolled along, black and sluggish, and with deep gurgling sounds under the wooden bridge. There was a single lamp there, with broken, dusty glass. Now and then the gleam of the light, which was blown uneasily hither and thither by the gusts of wind, would fall on a rippling wave below and dissolve on its crest. The rounded foot-planks of the bridge yielded under every step . . . revolving forward, then back again. . . .

Beineberg stopped. The farther bank was thickly wooded, and along the road, which turned at a right-angle on the other side and continued along the river, the trees had the menacing look of a black, impenetrable wall. Only if one looked carefully did one discover a narrow, hidden path leading straight on and into it. As, they went on their way through the thick, rank under-growth, which brushed against their clothes, they were continually showered with drops. After a while they had to stop again and strike a match. It was very quiet now ; even the gurgling of the river could not be heard. Suddenly from the distance there came a vague, broken sound. It was like a cry or a warning. Or perhaps it was merely like a call from some inarticulate creature that, somewhere ahead, was breaking its way through the bushes, like themselves. They walked on towards this sound, stopped again, and again walked on. All in all it was perhaps a quarter of an hour before, with a long breath of relief, they recognized loud voices and the notes of a concertina.

Now the trees grew more sparsely, and a few paces further they found themselves standing on the edge of a clearing, in the midst of which there was a squat, square building, two storeys high.

It was the old pump-room. In former times it had been used by the people of the little town and peasants from the neighbouring countryside for taking the waters ; but for years now it had been almost empty. Only the ground floor was still used, as a tavern, and one that was of ill repute.

The two boys stopped for a moment, listening.

Törless was just taking a step forward, about to issue forth from the thicket, when there was a sound of heavy boots tramping on the floor-boards inside the house and a drunken man came staggering out of the door. Behind him, in the shadow of the doorway, stood a woman, and they could hear her whispering hurriedly and angrily, as though demanding something from the man. He merely laughed, swaying on his feet. Then it seemed that the woman was pleading, but again the words were indistinguishable ; all that could be made out was the coaxing, cajoling tone of the voice. Now she advanced further and laid a hand on the man's shoulder. The moon shone upon her, lighting up her petticoat, her jacket, her pleading smile. The man stared straight ahead of him, shook his head, and kept his hands firmly in his pockets. Then he spat and pushed the woman away, perhaps because of something she had said. Now their voices were raised and what they said could be understood.

" —so you won't pay up, eh ? You—— ! "

" You just take yourself off upstairs, you dirty slut ! "

" The cheek ! You peasant clod, you ! "

By way of answer the drunken man bent down, with a clumsy movement, and picked up a stone. " If you don't clear off, you silly bitch, I'll knock your block off ! ", and he raised his arm, preparing to throw the stone at her. Törless heard the woman running up the steps with a last cry of abuse.

The man stood still for a moment, irresolutely holding the stone in his hand. He laughed, glanced up at the sky, where the moon floated, wine-yellow, among black clouds, and then stared at the dark mass of the thicket, as though he were wondering whether to go that way. Warily Törless drew his foot back ; he could feel his heart hammering in his throat. Finally, however, the drunken man seemed to reach a decision. The stone dropped from his hand. With a raucous, triumphant laugh he shouted an obscenity up at the window ; then he disappeared round the corner.

The two boys stood motionless a while longer. " Did you recognise her ? " Beineberg whispered. " It was Božena." Törless did not answer ; he was listening, trying to make sure that the drunken man was not coming back again. Then Beineberg gave him a push forward. In swift, wary dashes—avoiding the wedge of light from the ground-floor window—they crossed the clearing and entered the dark house. A wooden staircase, narrow and twisting, led up to the first floor. Here their footsteps must have been heard, or perhaps the clatter of their swords against the woodwork, for the door of the tavern room opened and someone came out to see who was in the house ; at the same time the concertina ceased playing, and there was a momentary hush in the talk, a pause of suspense.

Startled, Törless pressed close to the staircase wall. But in spite of the darkness it seemed he had been seen, for he heard the barmaid's jeering voice as the door was shut again, and whatever she said was followed by guffaws of laughter.

On the first-floor landing it was pitch-dark. They hardly dared to take another step for fear of knocking something over and making a noise. Fumbling excitedly, they felt their way along towards the door-handle.

*   *   *

As a peasant girl Božena had gone to the capital, where she went into service and in time became a lady's maid.

At first she did quite well. Her peasant ways, which she never entirely lost any more than her plodding, firm-footed walk, inspired confidence in her mistresses, who liked the whiff of the cow-shed about her and the simplicity they associated with it ; it also inspired amorous desires in her masters, who liked the whiff of the cow-shed for other reasons. Perhaps from caprice, and perhaps too from discontent and a vague yearning for passion, sne gave up this quiet, orderly life. She took a job as a waitress, fell ill, found employment in a house of public resort, one of the smarter kind, and in the course of time, in the same measure as her debauched life wore her down, drifted further and further out into the provinces again.

And finally here, where she had now been living for several years, not far from her native village, she helped in the tavern during the day and spent the evenings reading cheap novels, smoking cigarettes, and occasionally having a man in her room.

She had not yet become actually ugly, but her face was strikingly lacking in any sort of charm, and she evidently went to some trouble to emphasise this by her general air and behaviour. She liked to convey that she was well acquainted with the smartness and the manners of the stylish world, but that she had got beyond all that sort of thing. She was fond of declaring that she did not care a snap of the fingers for that, or for herself, or indeed for anything whatsoever. On this account, and in spite of her blowsiness, she enjoyed a certain degree of respect among the peasant lads of the neighbourhood. True, they spat when they spoke of her, and felt obliged to treat her with even more coarseness than other girls, but at bottom they were really mightily proud of this ' damned slut ' who had issued from their own midst and who had so thoroughly seen through the veneer of the world. Singly and furtively, it is true, but ever and again they came to see her. Thus Božena found a residue of pride and self-justification in her life. But what gave her perhaps even greater satisfaction was the young gentlemen from ' the college '. For their benefit she deliberately displayed her crudest and most repellent qualities, because—as she was in the habit of putting it—in spite of that they still came creeping along to her just the same.

When the two friends came in she was, as usual, lying on her bed, smoking and reading.

Even as he hesitated in the doorway, Törless was greedily devouring her with his eyes.

" Bless my soul, look at the pretty boys that have come ! " she called out in scornful greeting, surveying them with a shade of contempt. " Well, young Baron ?

35

What'll Mamma say to this, eh?" This was the sort of welcome to be expected from her.

"Oh, shut up!" Beineberg muttered, sitting down on the bed beside her. Törless sat down at some distance ; he was annoyed with Božena for taking no notice of him and pretending she did not know him.

Visits to this woman had recently become his sole and secret delight. Towards the end of the week he would become restless, scarcely able to wait for Sunday, when he would steal off to her in the evening. It was chiefly this necessary stealth that preoccupied him. What, for instance, if the drunken yokels in the bar-room just now had taken it into their heads to pursue him? Say for the sheer pleasure of taking a swipe at the vicious young gentleman. . . . He was no coward, but he knew he was defenceless here. By comparison with those big fists his dainty sword was a mockery. And apart from that, the disgrace and the punishment that would follow! There would be nothing for it but to run, or to plead for mercy. Or to let himself be protected by Božena. The thought went shuddering through him. But that was it! That was just it! Nothing else! This fear, this self-abandonment, was what seduced him anew every time. This stepping out of his privileged position and going among common people—among them? no, lower than them!

He was not vicious. When it came to the point his repugnance always had the upper hand, and together with it his fear of possible consequences. It was only his imagination that had taken an unhealthy turn. When the days of the week began to lay themselves, leaden, one by one, upon his life, these searing lures began to work upon him. The memories of these visits gradually took on the character of a peculiar temptation. Božena appeared to him as a creature of monstrous degradation, and his relationship to her, with the sensations it evoked in him, was like a cruel rite of self-sacrifice. It fascinated him to have to break the bounds of his ordinary life, leaving behind his privileged position, the ideas and feelings with which he was, as it were, being injected, all those things that gave him nothing and only oppressed him. It fascinated him to throw everything to the winds and, shorn of it all, to go racing off crazily and take his refuge with this woman.

This was no different from the way it is with such young people generally. Had Božena been pure and beautiful and had he been capable of love at that time, he would perhaps have sunk his teeth in her flesh, so heightening their lust to the pitch of pain. For the awakening boy's first passion is not love for the one, but hatred for all. The feeling of not being understood and of not understanding the world is no mere accompaniment of first passion, but its sole non-accidental cause. And the passion itself is a panic-stricken flight in which being together with the other means only a doubled solitude.

Almost every first passion is of short duration and leaves a bitter after-taste. It is a mistake, a disappointment. Afterwards one cannot understand how one could ever have felt it, and does not know what to blame for it all. That is because the characters in this drama are to a large extent accidental to each other : chance companions on some wild flight. When everything has calmed down, they no longer recognise each other. They become aware of discordant elements in each other, since they are no longer aware of any concord.

With Törless it was different only because he was alone. The ageing and degraded prostitute could not release all the forces in him. Yet she was woman enough to, as it were, bring to the surface, prematurely, particles of his innermost being, of all that still lay dormant in him waiting for the moment of fulfilment.

Such, then, were his weird imaginings and fantastic temptations. But at times he was almost as ready to fling himself on the ground, screaming with desperation.

* * *

Božena was still taking no notice of Törless. She seemed to be behaving in this way out of spite, merely in order to annoy him. Suddenly she broke the talk off by saying : " Give me some money, you boys, I'll fetch tea and gin."

Törless gave her one of the silver coins that had been a present from his mother that afternoon.

She took a battered spirit-lamp from the window-sill and lit it. Then she went out, slowly shuffling down the stairs.

Beineberg nudged Törless. "Why are you being such a bore ? She'll think you're scared."

" Leave me out of it," Törless said. " I'm not in the mood. You go ahead and have your fun with her. By the way, why does she keep on about your mother like that ? "

" Since she's known my name she insists she was once in service with my aunt and knew my mother. I dare say there's some truth in it, but I'm sure the rest is a lie —she *likes* lying. Anyway, I can't quite see what the joke is."

Törless blushed. A strange thought had just occurred to him. But at that moment Božena came back with the gin and sat down on the bed again beside Beineberg. And she at once took the conversation up where it had been dropped.

" Yes, your Mamma was a good-looking girl. You don't take after her very much, really, with those ears of yours sticking out like that. She was a gay one, too. There were plenty of men after her, I dare say. How right she was."

After a pause, something particularly amusing seemed to occur to her. "You know your uncle, the dragoon officer . . . Karl was his name, I think, he was a cousin of your mother's. How he did pay court to her! But on Sundays, when the ladies were in church, he was after me. Every few minutes I had to be bringing something to his room for him. A stylish chap he was, I remember him well, but he didn't beat around the bush much, I must say . . ." And she laughed insinuatingly. Then she continued elaborating this theme, which apparently afforded her particular pleasure. Her manner of speech was impertinently familiar, and her tone was even more scurrilous than her words. " . . . It's my guess your mother had a liking for him too. If she'd only known about the goings-on! I dare say your aunt would have had to kick me out of the house, and him too. That's the way fine ladies are, and all the more when they haven't got a man yet. Dear Božena here and dear Božena there—that's the way it went all day long. But when the cook got in the family way, my word, you should have heard them! I'm sure what they think about the like of us is that we only wash our feet once a year. Not that they said a word to the cook, but I heard plenty when I happened to be in the room and they happened to be talking about it. Your mother looked as if she felt like drinking nothing but eau-de-Cologne. And for all that it wasn't so long before your aunt herself had a belly on her so big it nearly touched her nose. . . ."

While Božena was talking, Törless felt almost totally defenceless against her coarse innuendos.

He could see vividly before his eyes what she was describing. Beineberg's mother turned into his own.

39

He remembered the bright rooms at home; the well-cared-for, immaculate, unapproachable faces that often inspired him with a certain awe when his parents gave dinner-parties; the cultivated, cool hands that seemed to lose none of their dignity even while handling knife and fork. Many such details came back to his mind, and he was ashamed of being here in a malodorous little room, trembling whenever he replied to the humiliating words uttered by a prostitute. His memory of the perfected manners of that society, which never for an instant allowed itself any slip out of its own style, had a stronger effect on him than any moral considerations. The up-heaval of his dark passions suddenly seemed ridiculous. With visionary intensity he saw the cool gesture of rejection, the shocked smile, with which those people would brush him off, like a small, unclean animal. Nevertheless he remained sitting where he was, as though transfixed.

For with every detail that he remembered not only the shame grew greater in him, but with it a chain of ugly thoughts. It had begun when Beineberg explained what Božena was talking about and Törless had blushed.

At that moment he had suddenly found himself thinking of his own mother, and this now held him in its grip and he could not shake it off. At first it had simply shot across the frontiers of his consciousness—a mere flash of something, too far away to be recognised, on the very edge of his mind—something that could scarcely be called a thought at all. And immediately it had been followed by a series of questions that were meant to cover it up: ' What is it that makes it possible for this woman Božena to bring her debased existence into proximity with my mother's existence? To squeeze up against her in the narrow space of one and the same thought? Why does she not bow down and touch the ground with her forehead when she speaks of her, if she must speak of her at all? Why isn't it as plain as if there were an abyss between them that they have nothing whatsoever in common? How *can* it be like this?—this woman, who is for me a maze of all sexual lust, and my mother, who up to now moved through my life like a star, beyond the reach of all desire, in some cloudless distance, clear and without depths . . .'

But all these questions were not the core of the matter. They scarcely touched it. They were something secondary, something that occurred to Törless only afterwards. They multiplied only because none of them pointed to the real thing. They were only ways of dodging the real problem, circumlocutions for the fact that, all at once, preconsciously, instinctively, an association of feelings had come about that was an inimical answer to the questions even before they were formulated. Törless devoured Božena with his eyes, and at the same time was unable to put his mother out of his mind. It was his being that linked them one with another, inextricably; everything else was only a writhing under this convolution of ideas. This was the sole fact. But because he was unable to shake himself free of its tyranny, it assumed a terrible, vague significance that hovered over all his efforts like a perfidious smile.

*　　*　　*

Törless looked round the room, trying to rid himself of these thoughts. But by now everything had taken on the one aspect. The little iron stove with the patches of rust on the lid, the bed with the rickety posts and the paint peeling off the wooden frame, the dirty blankets showing through holes in the worn counterpane; Božena, with her shift slipping off one shoulder, the common, glaring red of her petticoat, and her broad, cackling

41

laughter; and finally Beineberg, whose behaviour by contrast with other times struck Törless as like that of a lecherous priest who had taken leave of his senses and was weaving equivocal words into the solemn formulæ of a prayer: all this was urgent in one and the same direction, invading him and violently turning his thoughts back again and again.

Only at one place did his gaze, which fled nervously from one thing to another, find rest. That was above the little curtain over the lower half of the window. There the sky looked in, with the clouds travelling across it, and the unmoving moon.

Then he felt as if he had suddenly stepped out of doors into the fresh, calm air of the night. For a while all his thoughts grew still. A pleasant memory came back to him: that of the house they had taken in the country the previous summer . . . nights in the silent grounds . . . a velvety dark firmament tremulous with stars . . . his mother's voice from the depths of the garden, where she was strolling on the faintly glimmering gravel paths, together with his father . . . songs that she hummed quietly to herself . . . But at once—a cold shudder went through him—there was again this tormenting comparison. What must the two of them have been feeling then? Love? The thought came to him now for the first time. But no, that was something entirely different. That was nothing for grown-up people, and least of all for his parents. Sitting at the open window at night and feeling abandoned by everyone, feeling different from the grown-ups, misunderstood by every laugh and every mocking glance, being unable to explain to anybody what one already felt oneself to be, and yearning for *her*, the one who would understand—that was love! But in order to feel that one must be young and lonely. With them it must have been something different, something calm and composed. Mamma simply hummed a little song there in the evening, in the dark garden, and was cheerful. . . .

But that was the very thing Törless could not understand. The patient plans that for the adult imperceptibly link the days into months and years were still beyond his ken. And so too was that blunting of perception which makes it cease to be anything of a problem when yet another day draws to its close. His life was focused on each single day. For him each night meant a void, a grave, extinction. The capacity to lay oneself down to die at the end of every day, without thinking anything of it, was something he had not yet acquired.

That was why he had always supposed there was something behind it that they were keeping from him. The nights seemed to him like dark gateways to mysterious joys that were kept a secret from him, so that his life remained empty and unhappy.

He recalled the peculiar ring of his mother's laughter and how, as he had observed on one of those evenings, she had clung more tightly, as though jokingly, to her husband's arm. There seemed to be no doubt. There must be a gate leading hither even out of the world of those calm and irreproachable beings. And now, since he knew, he could think of it only with that special smile of his, expressing the malicious mistrust against which he struggled in vain . . .

Meanwhile Božena had gone on talking. Törless began to listen with half an ear. She was talking about somebody who also came almost every Sunday. " Let me see now, what's his name? He's in your class."

" Reiting ? "

" No."

" What does he look like ? "

" He's about as tall as him over there," Božena said

43

with a jerk of her head in Törless's direction, " only
his head is a bit too big."

" Oh, Basini ? "

" Yes, that's right, that's what he said his name was.
He's really comical. And quite the fine gentleman,
drinks nothing but wine. But he's stupid. It costs
him a pretty penny, and he never does anything but tell
me stories. He boasts about the love-affairs he says
he has at home. What does he get out of it ? I can
see quite plainly it's the first time in his life he's been
with a woman. You're only a young lad too, but you've
got a nerve. But he's clumsy and frightened of it, and
that's why he spins his long-winded stories about how
to treat women if you're a sensualist—yes, that's what
he calls himself. He says women don't deserve anything else. How do the like of you know that so soon,
I wonder ? "

By way of answer Beineberg grinned at her mockingly.

" Oh all right, laugh if you like ! " Božena flung at him
in amusement. " One time I asked him if he wouldn't
be ashamed for his mother to know. ' Mother ?
Mother ? ' he said. ' What's that ? There's no such
thing now. I left that at home, before I came to see
you. . . .' Yes, you may well prick up your big ears,
that's what you boys are like ! Good little sons you
are, you fine young gentlemen ! It almost makes me
sorry for your mothers ! "

At these words Törless recalled his former notion of
himself, realising how he was leaving everything behind
him and betraying the image of his parents. And now he
had to admit to himself that in this he was not even doing
something unique and terrible ; it was really quite commonplace. He was ashamed. But the other thoughts
were there again too. They do it too ! They betray
you ! You have secret accomplices ! Perhaps it is

44

somehow different with them, but this one thing must be the same : a secret, frightful joy. Something in which one can drown oneself and all one's fear of the monotony of the days . . . Perhaps indeed they know more ? . . . something quite extraordinary ? For in the daytime they are so calm . . . And that laughter of his mother's ? . . . as though she were going, with quiet steps, to shut all the doors . . .

In this conflict there came a moment when Törless abandoned himself, letting the tempest rage over his suffocating heart.

And at that very moment Božena got up and came over to him.

"Why is our little boy not talking ? Miserable, eh ? "

Beineberg whispered something and smiled spitefully.

"Homesick, eh ? Mamma's gone away, has she ? And the moment she's gone the naughty boy comes running to the like of me ! "

Božena dug her fingers caressingly into his hair.

"Come on, don't be silly. Give me a kiss, that's right. You fine gentry are only made of flesh and blood, after all, the same as everyone else," and she bent his head back.

Törless wanted to say something, to pull himself together and utter some crude joke, for he felt that everything now depended on his being able to speak some indifferent word that would not betray him. But he could not utter a sound. With a stony smile he gazed into the depraved face, the blank eyes looking down into his own, and then the outer world began to shrink, to withdraw further and further. . . . For a moment there loomed before him the image of the peasant who had picked up the stone, and it seemed to jeer at him. Then he was quite alone.

"I SAY," Reiting whispered, "I've got him."

"Who?"

"The chap who's been stealing from the lockers!"

Törless had just come in, together with Beineberg. It was only a short time till supper, and the usher on duty had already left. Groups of chattering boys had formed between the green baize tables, and the whole large room hummed and whirred with warm life.

It was the usual class-room with whitewashed walls, a big black crucifix, and portraits of the Emperor and Empress on each side of the blackboard. Beside the large iron stove, which was not yet lighted, the boys sat—some of them on the platform, some of them on overturned chairs—among them those who had been at the railway station that afternoon to see Törless's parents off. Apart from Reiting they were the tall Hofmeier and Dschjusch, a little Polish count who was known by this nickname.

Törless felt a certain curiosity.

The lockers, which were at the back of the room, were long cupboards subdivided into compartments that could be locked, and in them the boys kept their letters, books, money, and all their little pet possessions.

For some time now various boys had been complaining that they had missed small sums of money, but none of them had anything definite to go on.

Beineberg was the first to be able to say with certainty that the previous week he had been robbed of a consider-

46

able sum of money.   But only Reiting and Törless knew of it.

They suspected the servants.

" Go on, tell us ! " Törless urged.

But Reiting made a swift sign to him.   " Sssh !   Later. Nobody knows anything about it yet."

" Servant ? " Törless whispered.

" No."

" Well, give us some idea, anyway.   Who ? "

Reiting turned away from the others and said in a low voice : " B."   No one else had heard anything of this whispered conversation.   Törless was thunderstruck at what he had learnt.   B. ?   That could only be Basini. And surely that wasn't possible !   His mother was a wealthy woman, and his guardian an ' Excellency '. Törless could not bring himself to believe it, and yet time and again the story Božena had told came to his mind.

He could scarcely wait for the moment when the others went in to supper.   Beineberg and Reiting remained behind, on the pretext of having had so much to eat that afternoon.

Reiting suggested that it would be better to go ' upstairs ' and talk about it there.

They went out into the corridor, which stretched endlessly in each direction outside the class-room.   The flickering gas-light lit it only in patches, and their footsteps echoed from recess to recess, however lightly they walked. . . .

About fifty yards from the door there was a staircase leading up to the second floor, where the natural science ' specimen ' room was, and other collections that were used in teaching.   There were also a large number of empty rooms.

From there on the stairs became narrow and went up,

47

in short flights at right-angles to each other, to the attics. And—as old buildings are often whimsical in plan, with an abundance of nooks and crannies and unmotivated steps—this staircase actually went a considerable way above the level of the attics, so that on the other side of the heavy, iron, locked door, which blocked the way further, it was necessary to go down again, by a flight of wooden steps, in order to reach the floor of the attic.

What this meant was that on this side of the attic door was waste space some yards high, reaching up into the rafters. In this place, which hardly anybody ever entered, old stage-scenery had been stored, dating from school theatricals in the remote past.

Even at brightest noon the daylight on this staircase was reduced to a twilight, which was choked with dust, for this way into the attic, lying as it did in a remote wing of the enormous building, was almost never used.

From the top landing Beineberg swung himself over the bannister and, still holding on to the bars, let himself drop between the pieces of scenery. Reiting and Törless followed him. There they got a footing on a crate that had been specially dragged along for that purpose, and from there jumped to the floor.

Even if the eye of someone standing on the stairs had become accustomed to the darkness, that person could not possibly have seen anything there but an irregular and indistinct jumble of variously shaped pieces of stage-scenery all piled up together.

But when Beineberg shifted one of these pieces of scenery slightly to one side, a narrow tunnel opened up before the boys.

They hid the crate that had aided them in their descent, and entered the tunnel.

Here it became completely dark, and one had to know one's way very well in order to make progress. Now and then one of the big pieces of canvas scenery rustled, when they brushed against it ; there was a scurrying on the floor as of startled mice ; and their nostrils were filled with a musty smell as though from long-unopened trunks.

The three boys, who knew the way well, nevertheless went along very cautiously, step for step, careful to avoid tripping on any of the ropes pulled tight across the floor as traps and alarm-signals.

It was some time before they reached a little door on their right, only a short distance from the wall separating this place from the attic.

When Beineberg opened this door they found themselves in a narrow room under the top landing. It looked fantastic enough in the light of a small, flickering oil-lamp, which Beineberg had lit.

The ceiling was horizontal only where it was directly under the landing, and even here only just high enough for one to be able to stand upright. Towards the back it sloped away, following the line of the stairs, until it ended in an acute angle. The thin partition-wall at the opposite side of the room divided the attic from the staircase, and the third wall was formed by the brick-work on which the stairs rested. It was only the fourth wall, in which the door was, that seemed to have been added specially. Doubtless it had been built with the intention of making a small room here to keep tools in, unless perhaps it owed its existence only to a whim on the part of the architect, in whom this dark nook had inspired the mediæval notion of walling it up to make a hiding-place.

However that might be, apart from these three boys there was doubtless scarcely anyone in the whole school who knew of its existence, and still less anyone who thought of putting it to any use.

And so they had been free to furnish it entirely according to their own fantastic notions.

The walls were completely draped with some blood-red bunting that Reiting and Beineberg had purloined from one of the store-rooms, and the floor was covered with a double layer of thick woolly horse-blanket, of the kind that was used in the dormitories as an extra blanket in winter. In the front part of the room stood some low boxes, covered with material, which served as seats ; at the back, in the acute angle formed by the sloping ceiling and the floor, a sort of bed had been made, large enough for three or four people, and this part could be darkened by the drawing of a curtain, separating it from the rest of the room.

On the wall by the door hung a loaded revolver.

Törless did not like this room. True, the constriction and isolation it afforded appealed to him ; it was like being deep inside a mountain, and the smell of the dusty old stage-scenery gave rise to all sorts of vague sensations in him. But the concealment, those trip-ropes to give the alert, and this revolver, which was meant to provide the utmost illusion of defiance and secrecy, struck him as ridiculous. It was as though they were trying to pretend they were leading the life of bandits.

Actually the only reason why Törless joined in was that he did not want to lag behind the other two. Beineberg and Reiting themselves took the whole thing very seriously indeed. Törless knew that. He also knew that Beineberg had skeleton keys that would open the doors of all the cellars and attics in the school building, and that he often slipped away from lessons for several hours in order to sit somewhere—high up in the rafters of the roof, or underground in one of the many semi-ruinous, labyrinthine vaults—by the light of a little lamp, which he always carried about with him, reading

adventure stories or thinking his thoughts about supernatural things.

He knew similar things of Reiting, who also had his
hidden retreats, where he kept secret diaries ; and these
diaries were filled with audacious plans for the future
and with exact records of the origin, staging, and course
of the numerous intrigues that he instigated among the
other boys. For Reiting knew no greater pleasure than
to set people against each other, subduing one with the
aid of the other and revelling in favours and flatteries
obtained by extortion, in which he could still sense the
resistance of his victim's hate.

" I'm practising," was the only excuse he gave, and he
gave it with an affable laugh. It was also by way of
practising that almost daily he would box in some out-
of-the-way place, against a wall, a tree, or a table, to
strengthen his arms and harden his hands with callouses.

Törless knew about all this, but he could understand it
only up to a certain point. He had several times accompanied both Reiting and Beineberg on their singular
paths. The fantastic element in it all did in fact appeal to
him. And what he also liked was afterwards coming
back into the daylight, walking among the other boys,
and being back in the midst of their jollity, while he
could still feel the excitements of solitude and the hallucinations of darkness trembling in his eyes and ears. But
when Beineberg or Reiting, for the sake of having someone to talk to about themselves, on such occasions
expounded what impelled them to all this, his understanding failed. He even considered Reiting somewhat
overstrung. For Reiting was particularly fond of talking
about how his father, who had one day disappeared, had
been a strangely unsettled person. His name was, as
a matter of fact, supposed to be only an incognito,
concealing that of a very exalted family. He expected

that his mother would make him acquainted with far-reaching claims that he would in due course put forward ; he had day-dreams of *coups d'état* and high politics, and hence intended to be an officer.

Törless simply could not take such ambitions seriously. The centuries of revolutions seemed to him past and gone once and for all. Nevertheless Reiting was quite capable of putting his ideas into practice, though for the present only on a small scale. He was a tyrant, inexorable in his treatment of anyone who opposed him. His supporters changed from day to day, but he always managed to have the majority on his side. This was his great gift. A couple of years earlier he had waged a great war against Beineberg, which ended in the defeat of the latter. Finally Beineberg had been pretty well isolated, and this although in his judgment of people, his coolness and his capacity for arousing antipathy against those who incurred his disfavour, he was scarcely less formidable than his opponent. But he lacked Reiting's charm and winning ways. His composure and his unctuous philosophic pose filled almost everyone with mistrust. One could not help suspecting something excessive and unsavoury at the bottom of his personality. Nevertheless he had caused Reiting great difficulties, and Reiting's victory had been little more than a matter of luck. Since that time they found it profitable to combine forces.

Törless, by contrast, remained indifferent to these things. Hence also he had no skill in them. Nevertheless he too was enclosed in this world and every day could see for himself what it meant to play the leading part in a State—for in such a school each class constitutes a small State in itself. Thus he had a certain diffident respect for his two friends. The urge he sometimes felt to emulate them, however, always remained a matter of dilettante experiment. Hence, and also because he was the younger, his relationship to them was that of a disciple or assistant. He enjoyed their protection, and they for their part would gladly listen to his advice. For Törless's mind was the most subtle. Once he was set on a trail, he was extremely ingenious in thinking out the most abstruse combinations. Nor was anyone else so exact as he in foreseeing the various possible reactions to be expected of a person in a given situation. Only when it was a matter of reaching a decision, of accepting one of these psychological possibilities as the definite probability and taking the risk of acting on it, did he fail, losing both interest and energy. Still, he enjoyed his role of secret chief of staff, and this all the more since it was practically the only thing that set him going, stirring him out of his state of deep inner boredom.

Sometimes, however, he did realise how much he was losing as a result of this psychological dependence. He was aware that everything he did was merely a game, merely something to help him over this time at school, this larval period of his existence. It was without relation to his real personality, which would emerge only later, at some time still a long way off in the future.

For when on certain occasions he saw how very seriously his two friends took these things, he felt quite unable to understand them. He would have liked to make fun of them, but still he could not help being afraid that there might be more truth behind their fantastic notions than he was capable of admitting to himself. He felt as though torn between two worlds : one was the solid everyday world of respectable citizens, in which all that went on was well regulated and rational, and which he knew from home, and the other was a world of adventure, full of darkness, mystery, blood, and un-dreamt-of surprises. It seemed then as though one excluded the other. A mocking smile, which he would have liked to keep always on his lips, and a shudder that ran down his spine cut across each other. What came about then was an incandescent flickering of his thoughts. . . .

Then he would yearn to feel something firm in himself at long last, to feel definite needs that would distinguish between good and bad, between what he could make use of and what was useless, and to know he himself was making the choice, even though wrongly—for even that would be better than being so excessively receptive that he simply soaked up everything. . . .

When he entered the little room this inner dichotomy had asserted itself in him again, as it always did here.

Meanwhile Reiting had begun telling what he had discovered.

Basini had owed him money and had kept on promising to pay and putting it off, each time giving his word of honour that he was really going to pay the next time. "Well, I didn't particularly mind that," Reiting commented. "The longer it went on, the more he was in my power. I mean, after all, breaking one's word three or four times is no joke, is it? But in the end I needed my money myself. I pointed this out to him, and he gave me his solemn oath. And of course didn't stick to it that time either. So then I told him I'd report him. He asked for two days' grace, as he was expecting supplies from his guardian. In the meantime, however, I did some investigating into his circumstances. I wanted to find out if he was in anyone else's power as well. After all, one must know what one has to reckon with.

"I wasn't particularly pleased with what I discovered. He was in debt to Dschjusch and to several of the others as well. He'd paid back some of it, and of course out of the money he still owed me. It was the others he

54

felt it most urgent to pay. That annoyed me. I wasn't going to have him thinking I was the easy-going one of the lot. I could scarcely have put up with that. But I thought to myself : ' Let's just wait and see. Sooner or later there'll be an opportunity to knock *that* sort of idea out of his head.' Once he mentioned the actual amount he was expecting, sort of casually, you know, to put my mind at rest by showing me it was more than what he owed me. So I checked up with the others and found out that the total amount he owed was far more than what he said he was expecting. ' Aha,' I thought to myself, ' so now I suppose he'll try it on yet once again.'

"And, sure enough, he came along to me, all confidentially, and asked me to give him a little more time, as the others were pressing him so hard. But this time I was dead cold with him. ' Beg off from the others,' I said to him, ' I'm not in the habit of taking a back seat.' So he said : ' I know you better, I trust you more.' ' You'll bring me the money tomorrow,' I said to him, ' or you'll have to comply with my terms. That's my last word.' ' What terms ? ' he wanted to know. Oh, you should have heard him ! As if he were prepared to sell his soul. ' What terms ? Oho ! You'll have to act as my vassal in all my enterprises.' ' Oh, if that's all, I'll do that all right, I'm *glad* to be on your side.' ' Oh no, not just when *you* happen to like it. You'll have to do everything I tell you to do—in blind obedience ! ' So now he squinted at me in a way that was half grinning and half embarrassed. He didn't know how far he ought to go, what he was letting himself in for, or how serious I was. Probably he would have promised me anything, but of course he couldn't help being afraid I was only putting him to the test. So in the end he got very red and said : ' I'll bring you the money.' I was getting my fun out of him, he'd turned out to be a fellow like that and I'd never taken any notice of him before, among the fifty others. I mean, he never sort of counted at all, did he? And now suddenly he'd come so close to me that I could see right into him, down to the last detail. I knew for a certainty the fellow was ready to sell himself —and without making much fuss about it, only so long as he could keep people from finding out. It was a real surprise, and there's no nicer sight than that : when a fellow is suddenly laid bare before you, and suddenly his way of living, which you've never troubled to notice before, is exposed to your gaze like the worm-holes you see when a piece of timber splits open. . . .

" Right enough, the next day he brought me the money. And that wasn't all, either. He actually invited me to have a drink with him down town. He ordered wine, cake, and cigarettes, and pressed it all on me—out of ' gratitude ', because I'd been so patient. The only thing about it I didn't like was how awfully innocent and friendly he acted. Just as if there'd never been an offensive word said between us. I said as much. But that only made him more cordial than ever. It was as if he wanted to wriggle out of my grip and get on equal terms with me again. He behaved as if it were all over and done with, and every other word he uttered was to assure me of his friendship. Only there was something in his eyes that was a sort of clutching at me as though he were afraid of losing this feeling of intimacy he had artificially worked up. In the end I was revolted by him. I thought to myself : ' Does he really think I'm going to put up with this ? ' and I began to think how I could take him down a peg or two. What I wanted was something that would really get under his skin. So then it struck me Beineberg had told me that morning that some of his money had been stolen. It just occurred to me by the way. But it kept coming back into my mind. And it made me feel quite tight about the throat. 'It *would* turn out wonderfully handy,' I thought to myself, and in a casual way I asked him how much money he had left. When he told me, I added it up and got the right answer. I laughed and asked him : 'Who on earth was so stupid as to lend you money again after all this ? ' 'Hofmeier,' he said.

"I simply shook with joy. The fact is, Hofmeier had come to me two hours before that, asking me to lend *him* some money. So what had shot into my head a few minutes ago suddenly turned out to be true. Just the way you think to yourself, merely as a joke : 'Now that house over there ought to go on fire,' and the next moment there are flames shooting out of it, yards high. . . .

"I quickly ran over all the possibilities in my mind once again. Admittedly there wasn't any way of making dead certain, but my instinct was good enough for me. So I leaned over towards him and said in the most amiable way you can imagine, just as if I were gently driving a little, thin, pointed stick into his brain : 'Look here, my dear Basini, why do you insist on trying to deceive me ? ' At that his eyes seemed to swim in his head with fear. And I went on : 'I dare say there are plenty of people you can take in, but I don't happen to be the right person. You know, don't you, that Beineberg . . .' He didn't turn red or white, it was as if he were waiting for some misunderstanding to be cleared up. 'Well, to cut a long story short,' I said, 'the money from which you've paid me back what you owed me is the money you took out of Beineberg's locker last night.'

"I leaned back to study the effect it had on him. He went as red as a tomato. He began spluttering and slavering, as though choked by his own words. Finally he managed to get it out. There were torrents of re-proaches and accusations against me. He wanted to know how I could dare to make such an assertion and what faintest justification there was for such an abominable conjecture. He said I was only trying to pick a quarrel with him because he was the weaker and that I was only doing it out of annoyance because now that he had paid his debts he was out of my power, and that he would appeal to the class—the ushers—the Head—and that God would bear witness to his innocence, and so on and on ad infinitum. I really began to be quite worried that I had done him wrong and hurt his feelings for nothing, he looked so sweet with his face all red. He looked just like a tormented, defenceless little animal, you know. Still, I couldn't bring myself to let it go at that quite so easily. So I kept up a jeering smile—almost only out of embarrassment, actually—as I went on listening to his talk. Now and then I wagged my head and said calmly : ' Yes, but I *know* you did.'

" After a while then he quieted down. I kept on smiling. I felt as though simply by smiling at him like that I could make a thief of him, even if he weren't one already. ' And as for putting it right again,' I thought to myself, ' there's always plenty of time for that later.'

" And then after a while, when he had kept on glancing at me furtively, he suddenly got quite white. A queer change came over his face. The innocent and delightful look that had beautified him vanished out of his face, so to speak together with the colour. It turned quite green, cheesy, and puffy. I've only seen anything like it once before—once in the street when I came along just as they were arresting a murderer. *He'd* been going around among people too, without anyone's noticing anything queer about him. But when the policeman put his hand on his shoulder, he was suddenly changed into a different person. His face altered and his eyes popped with terror and looked around, searching for some way of escaping—a thoroughgoing gallow's-bird he looked.

" That came back to my mind when the change came over Basini's face. Then I knew it all, and only had to bide my time. . . .

" And then it all came out. Without my having to say anything, Basini—worn out by my silence—began to blubber and implore me for mercy. He said he'd only taken the money because he was in a fix, and if I hadn't found him out he would have put it back before anyone noticed. He said I shouldn't say he'd *stolen* it. He'd only taken it as a secret loan. . . . By that time he was blubbering too much to say any more.

" Afterwards he began pleading with me again. He said he would do my will in everything, he would do whatever I wanted, if only I wouldn't give him away. At this price he positively offered to be my slave, and the mixture of cunning and greed and fear that wriggled in his eyes was simply disgusting. So to get it all done with I told him I'd think it over and decide what was to to be done with him, but I also told him that primarily it was Beineberg's affair. Well now, what do you chaps think we should do with him ? "

While Reiting told his story Törless listened in silence, with his eyes shut. From time to time a shiver went through him, right to his finger-tips, and in his head the thoughts rose to the surface, wildly and chaotically, like bubbles in boiling water. It is said to be thus with one who for the first time sets eyes on the woman who is destined to involve him in a passion that will be his undoing. It is said that between two human beings there can be a moment of bending down, of drawing strength from deep within, of holding breath—a moment of utmost inner tension under a surface of silence. No one can say what happens in this moment. It is, as it were, the shadow that coming passion casts ahead of it. This is an organic shadow ; it is a loosening of all previous tensions and at the same time a state of sudden, new bondage in which the whole future is already implicit ; it is an incubation so concentrated that it is sharp as the prick of a needle . . . And then again it is a mere nothing, a vague, dull feeling, a weakness, a faint dread . . .

That was how Törless felt it all. Reiting's story seemed to him, when he put it to himself squarely, to be of no importance in itself : a reckless misdeed, a mean and cowardly act, on Basini's side, and now, without doubt, some cruel whim of Reiting's would follow. On the other hand, however, he felt something like an anxious premonition that events had now taken a quite personal turn against himself and that there was in the incident some sharp menace directed against him, like a pointed weapon.

He could not help imagining Basini together with Božena, and he glanced around the narrow room. The walls seemed to threaten him, to be closing in on him, to be reaching out for him with blood-stained hands, and the revolver seemed to swing to and fro where it hung. . . .

Now for the first time it was as though something had fallen, like a stone, into the vague solitude of his dreamy imaginings. It was there. There was nothing to be done about it. It was a reality. Yesterday Basini had been the same as himself. Now a trap-door had opened and Basini had plunged into the depths. It was precisely as Reiting had described it : a sudden change, and the person had become someone else. . . .

And once again this somehow linked up with Božena.

He had committed blasphemy in his thoughts. The rotten, sweet smell rising from them had made him dizzy. And this profound humiliation, this self-abandonment, this state of being covered with the heavy, pale, poisonous leaves of infamy, this state that had moved through his dreams like a bodiless, far-off reflection of himself, all this had now suddenly *happened* to Basini.

So it was something one must really reckon with, something one must be on one's guard against, which could suddenly leap out of the silent mirrors in one's mind?

But then everything else was possible too. Then Reiting and Beineberg were possible. Then this narrow little room was possible . . . Then it was also possible that from the bright diurnal world, which was all he had known hitherto, there was a door leading into another world, where all was muffled, seething, passionate, naked, and loaded with destruction—and that between those people whose lives moved in an orderly way between the office and the family, as though in a transparent and yet solid structure, a building all of glass and iron, and the others, the outcasts, the blood-stained, the debauched and filthy, those who wandered in labyrinthine passages full of roaring voices, there was some bridge—and not only that, but that the frontiers of their lives secretly marched together and the line could be crossed at any moment. . . .

And the only other question that remained was : how is it possible? What happens at such a moment? What then shoots screaming up into the air and is suddenly extinguished?

These were the questions that this incident set stirring in Törless. They loomed up, obscurely, tight-lipped, cloaked in some vague, dull feeling . . . weakness . . . a faint dread . . .

And yet as though from a long way off, raggedly, at random, many of their words rang out within him, filling him with anxious foreboding.

It was at this moment that Reiting put his query.

Törless at once began to talk. In doing so he was obeying a sudden impulse, a rush of bewildered feeling. It seemed to him that something decisive was imminent, and he was startled by the approach of it, whatever it was, and wanted to dodge it, to gain time. . . . Even as he talked he could feel that he had nothing but irrelevant points to bring up, and that his words were without any inner substance, having nothing to do with his real opinion . . .

What he said was : " Basini is a thief." And the firm, hard ring of the last word pleased him so much that he repeated it twice. " A thief. And a thief gets punished —everywhere in the world. He must be reported. He must be expelled. If he reforms afterwards, that's his affair, but he doesn't belong here any more ! "

But Reiting, with a look of being unpleasantly disconcerted, said : "No, no, why go and rush to extremes ? "

" Why ? But isn't it a matter of course ? "

" Not at all. You're going on exactly as if fire and brimstone would be called down upon us all if we kept Basini in our midst a minute longer. It's not as if what he'd done were so very frightful, after all."

" How can you talk like that ! Do you really mean to sit, and eat, and sleep in the same room, day in, day out, with a creature who has stolen money and who's then gone and offered himself to you as your servant, your slave ? I simply fail to understand you. After all, we're being brought up together because we belong together socially. Will it be all the same to you if some day you find yourself in the same regiment with him, or working together in the same government office, if you meet him at the houses of people you know—supposing he were to pay court to your sister?"

"Here, I say, you *are* exaggerating!" Reiting said with a laugh. "Anyone would think we'd joined a fraternity for life! Do you really think we shall go round for ever wearing a badge: 'Educated at W. College for the Sons of Gentlemen—has special privileges and obligations '——? Afterwards each of us will go his own way, and everyone will become whatever he's entitled to become. There isn't only one society. So I don't think we need to worry about the future. And as for the present, I didn't say we've got to be dear friends with Basini. There'll be some way of managing all right so that a proper distance is kept. We've got Basini in the hollow of our hand, we can do whatever we like with him, for all I care you can spit at him twice a day. So long as he'll put up with it, what's to bother us about having him among us? And if he rebels, there's always time to show him who's master. . . . You've only got to drop the idea that there's any relationship between us and Basini other than the pleasure we get out of what a rotten swine he is!"

Although Törless was far from being convinced of his own line of argument, he pressed on with it. "Look here, Reiting, why are you so keen to defend Basini?"

"Keen to defend him? Not that I know of. I've no particular reason to defend him at all. The whole thing leaves me stone-cold from A to Z. I'm only annoyed at the way you exaggerate. What's the bee in your bonnet? Seems to be some kind of idealism. Enthusiasm for the sacred cause of the school, or for justice. You've no idea how boring and virtuous it sounds. Or perhaps "—and Reiting narrowed his eyes in suspicion—" you have some other reason for wanting Basini kicked out and only don't want to admit what

63

you're up to. Some old score to settle, eh? Well, come on, out with it! If there's enough in it we might really turn it to account."

Törless looked at Beineberg. But Beineberg only grinned. He sat there, cross-legged in Oriental style, sucking at a long chibouk, and with his protruding ears in this deceptive light he looked like a grotesque idol. "For all I care," he said, between puffs, "you chaps can do what you like. I'm not interested in the money, nor in justice either. In India they would drive a pointed bamboo pole through his guts. There'd be some fun in that, anyway. He's stupid and cowardly, so he would be no loss, and anyway it's always been a matter of the utmost indifference to me what happens to such people. They themselves are nothing, and what may yet become of their souls, we don't know. May Allah bestow his grace upon your verdict!"

Törless made no reply to this. After Reiting had disagreed with him and Beineberg had refused to take sides in the matter, leaving the decision to the two of them, he had no more to say. He did not feel capable of arguing further; indeed, he felt he no longer had any desire to do anything in order to prevent whatever was imminent.

And so a proposal that Reiting now put forward was accepted. It was resolved that for the present they should keep Basini under surveillance, appointing themselves, as it were, his guardians, in order to give him a chance to make good what he had done. His income and expenditure were from now on to be strictly checked and his relations with the rest of the boys to depend on permission from his three guardians.

This decision had the air of being very correct and benevolent. But this time Reiting did not say it was ' boring and virtuous '. For, without admitting it even to themselves, each of them was aware that this was to constitute only a sort of interim state. Reiting would have been reluctant to renounce any chance of carrying the affair further, since he got such pleasure out of it; on the other hand, however, he could not yet see clearly what turn he should give it next. And Törless was as though paralysed by the mere thought that from now on he would be in close touch with Basini every day.

When he had uttered the word 'thief' a short time earlier, for a moment he had felt easier. It had been like a turning out, a pushing away from himself, of the things that were causing such upheaval in him.

But the problems that instantly rose up again could not be solved by the use of this simple word. They had become more distinct, now that there was no longer any question of dodging them.

Törless glanced from Reiting to Beineberg, shut his eyes, repeated to himself the resolve that had just been made, and looked up again. . . . He himself no longer knew whether it was only his imagination that was like a gigantic distorting-glass between him and everything, or whether it was true and everything was really the way it uncannily loomed before him. And was it then only Beineberg and Reiting who knew nothing of these problems—and this although it was precisely the two of them who had from the beginning been so at home in this world that now all at once, for the first time, seemed so strange to him?

Törless felt afraid of them. But he felt afraid only as one might feel afraid of a giant whom one knew to be blind and stupid.

One thing, however, was settled : he was much further ahead now than he had been only a quarter of an hour earlier. There was no longer any possibility of turning back. A faint curiosity rose in him about what was to come, since he was held fast against his will. All that was stirring within him still lay in darkness, and yet he already felt a desire to gaze into this darkness, with all the shapes that populated it, which the others did not notice. There was a thin prickling chill mingled with this desire. It was as though over his life there would now always be nothing but a grey, veiled sky—great clouds, monstrous, changing forms, and the ever-renewed question : Are they monsters ? Are they merely clouds ?

And this question was for him alone ! A secret, strange territory forbidden to the others. . . .

So it was that Basini for the first time began to assume that significance which he was later to have for Törless.

THE next day Basini was put under surveillance.

It was done not without ceremony. It was in the morning, when they had slipped away from gymnastics, which were performed on a large lawn in the school grounds.

Reiting delivered a sort of speech. It was not exactly short. He pointed out to Basini that he had forfeited his right to exist, that he actually ought to be reported, and that it was only thanks to their extraordinary mercifulness that for the present they were sparing him the disgrace of expulsion.

Then he was informed of the particular conditions. Reiting took it upon himself to see that they were kept.

During the whole scene Basini was very pale, but did not utter a word, and his face revealed nothing of what was going on in him.

Törless found the scene alternately in very bad taste and of very great significance.

Beineberg's attention was focused on Reiting more than on Basini.

DURING the following days the affair seemed to be practically forgotten. Reiting was scarcely to be seen at all, except in class and at meals, Beineberg was more taciturn than ever, and Törless continually put off thinking about the matter.

Basini went around among the other boys just as if nothing had ever happened.

* * *

He was a little taller than Törless, but very slight in build, with slack, indolent movements and effeminate features. He was not very intelligent, and he was one of the worst at fencing and gymnastics, but he had a pleasing manner, a rather coquettish way of making himself agreeable.

His visits to Božena had begun only because he wanted to play the man. Backward as he was in his development, it was scarcely to be supposed that he was impelled by any real craving. What he felt was perhaps only a compulsion, a sort of obligation, lest he should be noticeably lacking in the aura of one who has had his experiences in gallantry. He was always glad when he left her, having got that behind him; all that mattered to him was to have the memory of it.

Occasionally, too, he lied—out of vanity. After every holiday, for instance, he came back with souvenirs of little affairs—ribbons, locks of hair, tiny *billets-doux*. But once, when he had brought back in his trunk a dear little scented, sky-blue garter, and it subsequently turned out to belong to none other than his own twelve-year-old sister, he was exposed to a great deal of jeering on account of his ridiculous boasting.

The moral inferiority that was apparent in him and his stupidity both had a single origin. He had no power of resisting anything that occurred to him and was always surprised by the consequences. In this he resembled the kind of woman, with pretty little curls on her forehead, who introduces doses of poison into her husband's food at every meal and then is amazed and horror-struck at the strange, harsh words of the public prosecutor and the death-sentence pronounced on her.

*   *   *

Törless avoided Basini. So there was a gradual fading of that profound inmost shock that had in the first instant gone to the roots of his thoughts, shaking his whole being. Things around him became rational again ; his sense of bewilderment left him and with each passing day the whole thing became more unreal, like vestiges of a dream, something that could not assert its existence in the real, solid world on which the sun shone.

In order to make still more sure of this condition, he wrote a letter all about it to his parents. The only thing he passed over in silence was what he himself had felt at the time.

He had now regained the point of view that it was after all best to get Basini expelled from school at the next opportunity. He simply could not imagine that his parents would think differently. What he expected from them was disgusted condemnation of Basini, a gesture of horror at his being in their son's proximity, something like the flick of the finger-tips with which one brushes off an unclean insect.

There was nothing of this kind in the letter he received by way of answer. His parents had been conscientious and painstaking about the matter, weighing up all the circumstances like sensible people, in so far as they could form a picture of it all from the rather incoherent and hasty letter he had written them. What appeared was that they inclined to the most indulgent and reserved judgment, and this all the more since they saw the need to allow for a certain element of exaggeration in their son's account, born of youthful indignation. Hence they approved of the decision to give Basini a chance to reform, and suggested that a person's career should not be ruined at the outset because of one minor offence, especially—and this, as was proper, they particularly emphasised—since those concerned were not mature adults, but at a stage when their characters were still unformed and undergoing development. It was doubt-less best, of course, to treat Basini in a strict and serious way, but at the same time one should be charitable in one's attitude to him and try to reform him.

They reinforced this by a whole series of examples, which were familiar to Törless. He distinctly remembered that in the junior classes, where the authorities favoured Draconic measures and kept pocket-money within strict limits, many of the little boys, in their natural greed for sweets and delicacies, often could not resist begging the fortunate possessor of a ham sandwich, or the like, for a piece of it. He himself had not always been proof against this temptation, even if, ashamed of it as he was, he tried to cover it up by abuse of the wicked, unkind school regulations. And he owed it not only to the passing of the years, but also to his parents' admonitions, as kindly as they were serious, that he had gradually learnt to have his pride and not to give in to such weaknesses.

But now all this failed to have any effect.

He could not help seeing that his parents were in many ways right, and he also knew that it was scarcely possible to judge quite accurately from such a distance ; yet something much more important seemed to be missing from their letter.

What was missing was any appreciation of the fact that something irrevocable had happened, something that ought never to happen among people in a certain stratum of society. What was missing was any sign of their being surprised and shocked. They treated it as though it were quite a normal thing, which must be handled with tact but without much ado, merely as a blemish, as something that was no more beautiful, but also no more avoidable, than the relief of one's natural needs. In their whole letter there was as little trace of any more personal feelings or dismay as there was in the attitude of Beineberg and Reiting.

Törless might usefully have taken some note of this too. Instead, however, he tore the letter into shreds and burnt it. It was the first time in his life that he committed such an act of disrespect towards his parents.

The effect on him was the opposite of what had been intended. In contrast with the plain view that had been set before him he was again suddenly filled with awareness of all that was problematic and ambiguous in Basini's crime. Shaking his head, he told himself that it still needed thinking about, although he could not give himself any exact account of the reason for this attitude.

It was queerest of all when he pursued the matter dreamily rather than with conscious thought. Then at one moment Basini seemed to him comprehensible, commonplace, and clear-cut, just as his parents and his friends seemed to see him : and the next moment this Basini would vanish, only to come again, and yet again, as a small and even smaller figure, tiny and sometimes luminous against a deep, very deep background. . . .

AND then one night—it was very late and everyone was asleep—Törless was waked by someone shaking him.

Beineberg was sitting on the edge of his bed. This was so unusual that he at once realised something extraordinary must be afoot.

"Get up. Don't make a noise, we don't want anyone to notice. I want you to come upstairs, I've got something to tell you."

Törless quickly put some clothes on, got into his slippers, and threw his coat round his shoulders.

When they were up in their lair, Beineberg put all the obstacles back in their places with special care. Then he made tea.

Törless, who was still heavy with sleep, relaxed in enjoyment of the golden-yellow, aromatic warmth pervading him. He leaned back in a corner and curled up; he was expecting a surprise.

At last Beineberg said: "Reiting is up to something behind our backs."

Törless felt no astonishment; he accepted it as a matter of course that the affair must necessarily develop in some such way, and he felt almost as though he had been waiting for this. Involuntarily he said: "I thought as much."

"Oh? You thought so, did you? But I don't suppose you noticed anything? That wouldn't be at all like you."

"That's true, there wasn't anything special that struck

me. And I haven't been racking my brains about the whole thing."

"But *I*'ve been keeping a good look-out. I didn't trust Reiting from the very beginning. I suppose you know Basini's paid me back my money. And where do you think he got it? D'you think it was his own? No."

"And so you think Reiting has been up to something?"

"Definitely."

For a moment all Törless could imagine was that now Reiting had got entangled in a similar way himself.

"So you think Reiting has done what——?"

"What an idea! Reiting simply gave Basini some of his own money, so that he could settle his debt to me."

"But I can't see any good reason why he should do that."

"Neither could I for a long time. Still, it must have struck you too how Reiting stood up for Basini right from the start. You were quite right then. It would really have been the most natural thing to have had the fellow chucked out. But I knew what I was doing. I didn't take your side at the time, because I thought to myself: I must get to the bottom of this, I must see what he's up to. Frankly, I can't say for certain whether he had it all worked out quite clearly at that stage or whether he only wanted to wait and see what would come of it once he made completely sure of Basini. Anyway, I know how things stand now."

"Well?"

"Wait, the whole story isn't so simple. I take it you know about what happened in the school four years ago?"

"What do you mean?"

"Well—that affair!"

" Vaguely.   I only know there was a great row about some swinishness that had been going on, and quite a number of chaps got expelled."

" Yes, that's what I mean.   Once in the holidays I found out some more about it from one of the chaps in that class.   It was all because of a pretty boy there was in the class, that a lot of them were in love with.   You know that sort of thing, it happens every few years. But *they* went a bit too far."

" How do you mean ? "

" Well—how !   Don't ask such silly questions !   And that's what Reiting's doing with Basini ! "

Törless suddenly understood what he meant, and he felt a choking in his throat as if it were full of sand.

" I wouldn't have thought that of Reiting."   He did not know what else to say.

Beineberg shrugged his shoulders.   " He thinks he can take us in."

" Is he in love with him ? "

" Not a bit of it.   He's not such a fool.   It amuses him ; at the most he gets some sort of excitement out of it."

" And how about Basini ? "

" Oh, him !   Hasn't it struck you how uppish he's become recently ?   He hardly takes anything from me at all now.   It's always Reiting, Reiting, with him—as if Reiting were his private patron saint.   He probably decided it was better to put up with everything from one than with a bit from everyone.   And I dare say Reiting's promised to look after him as long as he does whatever Reiting wants of him.   But they'll find out they've made a mistake, and I'm going to knock such ideas out of Basini's head ! "

" How did you find out ? "

" I followed them once."

"Where to?"

"In there, in the attic. Reiting had my key to the other door. Then I came up here, carefully opened up the gap and crept up to them."

The fact was that in the thin partition-wall dividing the cubby-hole from the attics they had broken open a gap just wide enough to allow one to wriggle through. It was intended to serve as an emergency exit in the event of their being surprised, and it was generally kept closed with loose bricks.

Now there was a long pause, in which all that could be heard was the faint hiss when the tips of their cigarettes glowed.

Törless was incapable of thinking; he simply saw . . . Behind his shut eyelids there was all at once a wild vortex of happenings . . . people, people moving in a glare, with bright lights and shifting, deep-etched shadows . . . faces . . . one face . . . a smile . . . an upward look . . . a shivering of the skin . . . He saw people in a way he had never seen them before, never felt them before. But he saw them without seeing, without images, without forms, as if only his soul saw them; and yet they were so distinct that he was pierced through and through by their intensity. Only, as though they halted at a threshold they could not cross, they escaped him the moment he sought for words to grasp them with.

He could not stop himself from asking more. His voice shook. "And—did you see?"

"Yes."

"And—did Basini—was he——?"

But Beineberg remained silent, and once again there was nothing to be heard but, now and then, the vaguely disturbing hiss of the cigarettes. Only after a long time did Beineberg begin to talk again.

"I've considered the whole thing from all points of view, and, as you know, I have my own way of thinking about such things. First of all, as far as Basini goes, it's my view he's no loss in any case. It makes no difference whether we go and report him, or give him a beating, or even if we torture him to death, just for the fun of it. Personally, I can't imagine that a creature like that can have any meaning in the wonderful mechanism of the universe. He strikes me as being merely accidental, as it were a random creation outside the order of things. That's to say—even he must of course mean something, but certainly only something as undefined as, say, a worm or a stone on the road, the sort of things you never know whether to walk round or step on. In other words, they're practically nothing. For if the spirit of the universe wants one of its parts to be preserved, it manifests its will more clearly. In such a case it says 'no' and creates a resistance, it makes us walk round the worm and makes the stone so hard that we can't smash it without tools. And before we can get the tools, it has had time to interpolate resistances in the form of all sorts of tough little scruples, and if we get the better of them, well, that just shows that the whole thing has had another meaning all along.

"With a human being, it puts this hardness into his character, into his consciousness as a human being, into the sense of responsibility he has as a part of the spirit of the universe. And if a human being loses this consciousness, he loses himself. But if a human being has lost himself, abandoned himself, he has lost the special and peculiar purpose for which Nature created him as a human being. And this is the case in which one can be perfectly certain that one is dealing with something unnecessary, an empty form, something that has already long been deserted by the spirit of the universe."

77

Törless felt no inclination to argue. He was not even listening very attentively. He himself had never felt the need to go in for such a metaphysical train of thought, nor had he ever wondered how anyone of Beineberg's intellect could indulge in such notions. The whole problem had simply not yet risen over the horizon of his life.

Thus he made no effort to enquire into the possible meaning, or lack of meaning, of Beineberg's remarks. He only half listened.

One thing he did not understand, and that was how anyone could approach this matter in such a long-winded way. Everything in him quivered, and the elaborate formality with which Beineberg produced his ideas—wherever he got them from—seemed to him ridiculous and out of place; it irritated him.

But Beineberg continued calmly : " Where Reiting is concerned, on the other hand, it's all very different. He has also put himself in my power by doing what he has done, but his fate is certainly not so much a matter of indifference to me as Basini's is. You know his mother is not very well off. So if he gets expelled, it'll be all up with his plans. If he stays here, he may get somewhere. If not, there's not likely to be much chance for him. And Reiting never liked me—see what I mean ?— he's always hated me. He used to try to damage me wherever he could. I think he would still be glad if he could get rid of me. Now do you see what an immense amount I can make out of what I've discovered ? "

Törless was startled—and it was strangely as if Reiting's fate affected him personally, were almost his own. He looked at Beineberg in dismay. Beineberg had narrowed his eyes to a mere slit, and to Törless he looked like a great, weird spider quietly lurking in its web. His last words rang in Törless's ears with the coldness and clarity of an ultimatum.

Törless had not been following, had only known : Beineberg is talking about his ideas again, and they have nothing at all to do with the matter in hand . . . And now all at once he did not know how it had reached this point.

The web, which had, after all, been begun somewhere far off in a realm of abstractions, as he vaguely remembered, seemed to have contracted suddenly and with miraculous speed. For all at once it was there, concrete, real, alive, and there was a head twitching in it—choking.

He was far from having any liking for Reiting, but he now recalled the agreeable, impudent, carefree way in which he set about all his intrigues, and in contrast Beineberg seemed infamous as he sat there, calm and grinning, pulling his many-threaded, grey, abominable web of thoughts tight around the other.

Involuntarily Törless burst out : " You mustn't turn it to account against him ! " What impelled him to the exclamation was perhaps partly his constant secret repugnance for Beineberg.

But after a few minutes' reflection Beineberg said of his own accord : " What good would it do, anyway ? Where he is concerned it would really be a pity. From now on in any case he's no danger to me, and after all he's not so worthless that one should trip him up over a silly thing of this kind." And so that aspect of the affair was settled. But Beineberg went on talking, now again turning his attention to Basini's fate.

" Do you still think we ought to report Basini ? "

But Törless gave no answer. Now he wanted Beineberg to go on talking, to hear his words sounding like the hollow echoing of footsteps over a vault ; he wanted to savour the situation to the full.

Beineberg went on expounding his ideas. " I think for the present we'll keep him in our own hands and

79

punish him ourselves. He certainly must be punished—
if only for his presumption. All the school would do
would be to send him home and write his uncle a long
letter about it. Surely you know more or less how
automatically that sort of thing works. Your Excellency,
your nephew has so far forgotten himself . . . bad influence . . . restore him to your care . . . hope you will
be successful . . . road towards improvement . . . for
the present, however, impossible among the others . . .
and so on and so forth. You don't suppose, do you,
that such a case has any interest or value in their eyes ? "

"And what sort of value can it have for us ? "

"What sort of value ? None for you, perhaps, for
you're going to be a government official some day, or
perhaps you'll write poems—all in all you don't need
that kind of thing, and perhaps you're even frightened
of it. But I picture my life rather differently."

Now Törless really began to listen.

"For me Basini has some value—very great value
indeed. Look, it's like this—you would simply let him
go and would be quite satisfied with the thought that he
was a bad person." Here Törless suppressed a smile.
"That's all it amounts to for you, because you have no
talent or interest in training yourself by means of such
a case. But I have that interest. Anyone with my road
ahead of him must take quite a different view of human
beings. That's why I want to save Basini up for myself
—as something to learn from."

"But how do you mean to punish him ? "

Beineberg withheld his answer for a moment, as though
considering the effect he expected it to have. Then he
said, cautiously and with some hesitation : "You're
wrong if you think I'm so very much concerned with the
idea of punishment. Of course ultimately it will be
possible to look at it as a punishment for him too. But

to cut a long story short, I've got something different in mind, what I want to do to him is—well, let's call it tormenting him."

Törless took good care to say nothing. He was still far from seeing the whole thing clearly, but he could feel that it was all working out as—inwardly—it must work out for him.

Beineberg, who could not gather what effect his words had had, continued : " You needn't be shocked, it's not as bad as all that. First of all, as I've already explained to you, there's no cause to consider Basini's feelings at all. Whether we decide to torment him or perhaps let him off depends solely on whether we feel the need of the one or the other. It depends on our own inner reasons. Have you got any ? All that stuff about morality and society and the rest of it, which you brought up before, doesn't count at all, of course. I should be sorry to think you ever believed in it yourself. So I assume you to be indifferent. But however it may be, you can still withdraw from the whole affair if you don't want to take any risks.

" My own road, however, leads not back or around, but straight ahead and through the middle of it. It has to be like that. Reiting won't leave off either, for in his case too there's a special value in having a human being in the hollow of his hand so that he can use him for the purpose of training himself, learning to handle him like a tool. He wants to exercise power, and he would treat you just the same as Basini if he ever happened to get the chance. But for me it's a matter of something more than that. It's almost a duty to myself. Now, how am I to make clear to you exactly what this difference is between him and me ? You know how Reiting venerates Napoleon. Now contrast that with the fact that the sort of person who most appeals to me is more like a philosopher or a holy man in India. Reiting would sacrifice Basini and feel nothing but a certain interest in the process. He would dissect him morally in order to find out what one has to expect from such operations. And, as I said before, it could be you or me just as well as Basini, and it would be all the same to him. On the other hand, I have this certain feeling, just as you have, that Basini is, after all, in the last resort a human being too. There's something in me too that is upset by any act of cruelty. But that's just the point! The point is the sacrifice! You see, there are two threads fastened to me too. The first is an obscure one that, in contrast with my clear conviction, ties me to the inaction that comes from pity. But there is the second, too, which leads straight to my soul, to the most profound inner knowledge, and links me to the universe. People like Basini, as I told you before, signify nothing—they are empty, accidental forms. True human beings are only those who can penetrate into themselves, cosmic beings that are capable of that meditation which reveals to them their relationship to the great universal process. These people do miracles with their eyes shut, because they know how to make use of the totality of forces in the universe, which are within them just as they are also outside them. But hitherto everyone who has followed up the second thread, has had to tear the first. I've read about appalling acts of penance done by illumined monks, and the means used by Indian ascetics are, I imagine, not entirely unknown to you either. All the cruel things that are done in this way have only one aim, to kill the miserable desires directed towards the external world, which, whether they are vanity or hunger, joy or pity, only take away something from the fire that everyone can kindle in himself.

"Reiting knows only the outward thread, but I follow

the second. For the present he has got ahead of me in everybody else's eyes, for my road is slower and more uncertain. But I can overtake him with one stride, just as if he were a worm. You see, they say the universe is governed by mechanical laws that are unshakable. That's all wrong! That's only what the school-books say! The external world is stubborn, I dare say, and to some extent its so-called laws stand firm, but there have been people who succeeded in bending them to their will. It's written about in sacred books that have stood the test of time and of which most people know nothing. From these books I know there have been people who could move stones and air and water merely by means of their will, and whose prayers were stronger than any earthly power. But even these are only the external triumphs of the spirit. For him who *entirely* succeeds in beholding his own soul, physical life, which is only an accidental thing, dissolves. It is written in the books that such beings enter directly into a higher spiritual realm."

Beineberg spoke with entire seriousness and with suppressed excitement. Törless still kept his eyes shut almost all the time ; he could feel Beineberg's breath like something touching him and drew it into himself like a suffocating narcotic. And so Beineberg concluded his harangue :

" Well, you can see what I am concerned with. What tells me to let Basini off is something of low, external origin. You can obey it if you like. For me it is a prejudice from which I have to cut myself loose as from everything else that would distract me from my inner way.

" The very fact that I find it hard to torture Basini— I mean, to humiliate him, debase him, and cast him away from me—is good. It requires a sacrifice. It will have a purifying effect. I owe it to myself to learn daily, with him as my material, that merely being human means nothing—it's a mockery, a mere external semblance."

Törless did not understand all of it. But once again it seemed to him as though an invisible noose had suddenly been tightened into a palpable and fatal knot. Beineberg's final words went on echoing in his mind: ". . . a mockery, a mere external semblance." It seemed to apply also to his own relation to Basini. Was it not in such fantasies that the queer fascination lay which Basini held for him? Was it not simply in the fact that he could not enter into Basini's mind and so always experienced him only in vague images? Just now, when he had tried to picture Basini to himself, had there not been behind his face a second one, blurred and shadowy and yet of a tangible likeness, though it was impossible to say what it was a likeness of?

So it came about that, instead of thinking over Beineberg's very odd intentions, being bemused as he was by these new and unfamiliar impressions, Törless was engaged in trying to become clear about himself. He remembered the afternoon before he had heard about Basini's offence. Come to think of it, these fantasies had been there even then. There had always been something that his thoughts could not get the better of, something that seemed at once so simple and so strange. There had been pictures in his mind that were not really pictures at all. It had been like that passing the cottages on the road back from the station, and also when he was sitting in the cake-shop with Beineberg.

They were likenesses and yet at the same time unlikenesses, unsurmountable. And the toying with it all, this secret, entirely private perspective, had excited him.

And now a human being took possession of this. Now it was all embodied in a human being; it had become real. Thus all the queerness of it attached itself to that human being. Thus it shifted out of the imagination into life itself and became a menace.

All this agitation had tired Törless; his thoughts were now but loosely linked together.

The only thing he could really hold on to was the thought that he must not let go of this Basini, that Basini was destined to play an important part in his life too, one that he already recognised, although as yet unclearly.

And yet, recalling Beineberg's words, he could not help shaking his head in amazement. Was it the same with him . . . ?

' It can't be that he is after the same things as I am, and yet it was he who found the right words for it . . .'

Törless was dreaming rather than thinking. He was no longer capable of distinguishing his own inner problem from Beineberg's flights of fancy. In the end nothing remained but the one feeling : a vast noose tightening, tightening round everything . . .

No more was said between them. They put out the light and crept warily back to their dormitory.

THE next days brought no decision. There was a great deal of school work, Reiting was careful not to find himself alone with either of them, and Beineberg too avoided any reopening of their last discussion.

So it happened, in the days that followed, that the thought of the affair went deeper into Törless, like a river forced underground, and set his imagination moving irrevocably in one particular direction.

This put a definite end to any intention of getting rid of Basini. Now for the first time Törless felt he was focused exclusively on himself, and was incapable of thinking of anything else. Božena too had become a matter of indifference to him. What he had felt about her now became a mere fantastic memory; it had been replaced by something really serious.

Admittedly, this really serious matter seemed no less fantastic.

*   *   *

Absorbed in his thoughts, Törless had gone for a walk alone in the park. It was noon, and in the light of the late autumn sun the lawns and paths shone as though with the wan gleam of memory. Since in his restlessness he felt no inclination to go far, he merely walked round the building and then threw himself down on the pale, rustling grass at the foot of an almost windowless side-wall. The sky above him was a vault—of that faded, ailing blue which is peculiar to autumn, and there were little white puffs of cloud scudding across it.

Lying flat on his back, he blinked, vaguely and dreamily, looking up between the tops of two trees in front of him, now almost leafless.

He thought about Beineberg. What a strange fellow that was! His way of talking would not have been out of place in some crumbling Indian temple, among uncanny idols, where wizard serpents lay hidden in deep crannies. But what place had such talk in broad daylight, in this school, in modern Europe? And yet those words of his, after trailing on and on, like an endless road of a thousand meanderings, leading no one knew where, had seemed suddenly to arrive at a tangible goal . . .

And suddenly—and it seemed to him as if it had happened for the very first time—Törless became aware of how incredibly high the sky was.

It was almost a shock. Straight above him, shining between the clouds, was a small, blue hole, fathomlessly deep.

He felt it must be possible, if only one had a long, long ladder, to climb up and into it. But the further he penetrated, raising himself on his gaze, the further the blue, shining depth receded. And still it was as though some time it must be reached, as though by sheer gazing one must be able to stop it and hold it. The desire to do this became agonisingly intense.

It was as if, straining to the utmost, his power of vision were shooting glances like arrows between the clouds; and yet, the further and further it aimed, still they always fell just a little short.

Now Törless began to think about this, making an effort to be as calm and rational as he could. " Of course there *is* no end," he said to himself, " it just keeps going on and on for ever, into infinity." He kept his eyes fixed on the sky, saying this aloud to himself as though

87

he were testing the power of a magical formula. But it was no use; the words meant nothing, or rather, they meant something quite different, as if, while dealing with the same subject, they were taking it from another side, one that was strange, unfamiliar and irrelevant.

"Infinity!" Törless had often heard the word in mathematics lessons. It had never meant anything in particular to him. The term kept on recurring; somebody had once invented it, and since then it had become possible to calculate with it as surely as with anything real and solid. It was whatever it stood for in the calculation; and beyond that Törless had never sought to understand it.

But now it flashed through him, with startling clarity, that there was something terribly disturbing about this word. It seemed to him like a concept that had been tamed and with which he himself had been daily going through his little circus tricks; and now all of a sudden it had broken loose. Something surpassing all comprehension, something wild and annihilating, that once had been put to sleep by some ingenious operation, had suddenly leapt awake and was there again in all its terrifying strength. There, in the sky, it was standing over him, alive and threatening and sneering.

At last he shut his eyes, the sight of it was such anguish to him.

*   *   *

When a little later he was aroused by a gust of wind rustling through the withered grass, he could scarcely feel his own body: there was a pleasant coolness streaming upwards from his feet, enfolding his limbs in gentle numbness. Now a kind of mild exhaustion mingled with his dismay. He still felt the sky as something vastly and silently staring down at him, but now he remembered how often before he had felt the same thing ; and in a state between waking and dreaming he went back through all those memories, feeling how they spun their threads round him, wrapping him up in ever further meanings and associations, as in a cocoon.

There was, first of all, that childhood memory of the trees standing there as solemn and silent as if they were really people under an enchantment. Even then he must have felt this thing that was later to happen to him again and again. There had been something of this even behind those thoughts he had had in Božena's room, something special, something of a larger pre-monition, that was more than the thoughts themselves. And that moment in the cake-shop when everything had grown quiet outside the window, in the garden, just before the dark veils of sensuality sank about him, yes, that too had been the same. And often, for the fraction of a thought, Beineberg and Reiting would turn into something strange, unfamiliar, unreal. And what about Basini ? The thought of what was happening to Basini had rent Törless in two. At one moment this thought was rational and commonplace ; at another it was vested in that same silence, flashing with sudden mental images, which was common to all these impressions, which had been steadily seeping through into Törless's conscious mind and which now all at once was asserting its claim to be treated as something real and living : just as the idea of infinity had, a while earlier.

Törless now felt it enclosing him on all sides. Like some far-off, obscure force it had probably been threaten-ing from the very beginning, but he had instinctively shrunk from it, only now and then giving it a shy, fleet-ing glance. But now a chance happening had made him alert to it, forced him to attend to it, and, as at a signal, it came rushing at him from all directions : a torrent of immense perplexity that spread out further and further with every instant.

Törless was assailed by a sort of madness that made him experience things, processes, people, all as something equivocal : as something that by some ingenious operation had been fettered to a harmless explanatory word and which nevertheless was something entirely strange, which might break loose from its fetters at any moment now.

True, there is a simple, natural explanation for everything, and Törless knew it too ; but to his dismayed astonishment it seemed only to tear off an outer husk, without getting anywhere near laying bare what was within—that other, further thing which now, as with a gaze that had grown unnaturally penetrating, he could always see glimmering underneath.

So he lay there, all wrapped up in memories, out of which strange notions grew like exotic flowers. Those moments that nobody forgets, when there is a failure of that power of association which generally causes our life to be faultlessly reflected in our understanding, as though life and understanding ran parallel to each other and at equal speed—those moments formed a bewilderingly close-knit mesh around him.

In his memory that dreadfully still, sad-coloured silence of certain evenings alternated abruptly with the hot, quivering uneasiness of a summer noon—an uneasiness that had once rippled over his soul, in blazing heat and as with the light flitting feet of innumerable iridescent lizards.

Then suddenly he recalled that little prince—his smile, the glance, the movement—with which, at the time when they had reached the end of their relationship, he had gently freed himself from all the associations that Törless had involved him in, and moved off into some distance—new and alien and, as it were, concentrated in the life of one ineffable instant—that had all at once opened out before him. Then again there came memories of the forest and from out in the fields. Then there was a silent scene in a darkening room at home, where he had suddenly felt reminded of his lost friend. Words of a poem came into his mind. . . .

And there are yet other things in which this incomparability reigns, somewhere between experience and comprehension. Yet it is always of such a nature that what in one moment we experience indivisibly, and without question, becomes unintelligible and confused as soon as we try to link it with chains of thought to the permanent store of what we know. And what looks grand and remote so long as our words are still reaching out towards it from a long way off, later, once it has entered the sphere of our everyday activities, becomes quite simple and loses all its disturbing quality.

*   *   *

And so it was that all these memories all at once had the same mystery in common. As though they all belonged together, they stood before him so distinctly that it seemed he could almost take hold of them.

In their own time they had been accompanied by an obscure emotion of which he had taken little notice.

And it was this that he was trying to get at now. It occurred to him that once, when he had been standing with his father, looking at one of those landscapes, he had suddenly cried out : ' Oh, how beautiful it is ! '— and then been embarrassed when his father was glad. For he might just as easily have said: 'How terribly sad it is.' It was the failure of language that caused him anguish, a half-awareness that the words were merely accidental, mere evasions, and never the feeling itself.

And today he recalled the scene, recalled the words—very distinctly recalled the sense he had had of falsehood, though without knowing why or in what way. In memory his eye went over it all again. But time and again it returned without bringing relief. A smile of delight in the wealth of the thoughts that came to him, a smile that had gradually become more and more absent-minded, now slowly took on a just perceptible twist of pain. . . .

He felt the urge to search unceasingly for some bridge, some connection, some means of comparison, between himself and the wordless thing confronting his spirit.

But as often as he had put his mind at rest about any one idea, there would again be that incomprehensible objection : It's all a lie. It was as if he must work out an unending sum in long division with a recurring decimal in it, or as if he were skinning his fingers in the frantic struggle to undo an endless knot.

And finally he gave up. It all closed tightly round him, and the memories grew large, weirdly distorted.

He had raised his eyes to the sky again—as though he might yet by some fluke snatch its secret from it and, that once gained, guess what perplexed him everywhere. But he grew tired, and a feeling of profound loneliness closed over him. The sky kept silence. And Törless felt that under that immovable, dumb vault he was quite alone, a tiny speck of life under that vast, transparent corpse.

But it hardly frightened him any more at all. It was like an old, familiar pain that had at last spread even to the last limb.

It seemed to him as if the light had now become milky and shimmering, dancing before his eyes like a pallid, cold mist.

Slowly and warily he turned his head and glanced

92

about him to see if everything had really changed. His glance happened to pass over the grey, windowless wall behind him : it seemed to have leaned forward over him and to be looking at him in silence. From time to time there was a faint rustling in it, the sound of uncanny life awakening in the bricks and mortar.

It was the same faint rustling he had often listened to in the lair upstairs, when Beineberg and Reiting had raised the curtain on their fantastic world, and he had rejoiced in it as in the queer incidental music to a grotesque play.

But now the bright day itself seemed to have turned into an unfathomable lair, and the living silence closed in on Törless from all sides.

He could not turn his head away. Beside him, in a damp, shady corner, the ground was overgrown with colt's-foot, its broad leaves making fantastic lurking-places for slugs and snails.

Törless could hear the beating of his own heart. Then again there was a faint, whispering rustle that came and faded away. . . . And these sounds were the only things alive in a timeless world of silence.

THE next day Törless saw Beineberg and Reiting together, and he went and joined them.

"I've talked to Reiting," Beineberg said, "and it's all fixed. After all, you're not really interested in such things, are you?"

Törless felt something like anger and jealousy rising up in him at this sudden change; but he did not quite know whether to mention the nocturnal discussion in front of Reiting. "Well, you might have called me in on it," he remarked. "After all, I've as much say in the whole thing as you chaps have."

"Oh, we would have, my dear Törless," Reiting hastened to say, obviously wishing to have no unnecessary difficulties this time. "But you happened to have disappeared, and we assumed you'd agree. Well, and what do you think of Basini now?" (There was no word of excuse, just as if his own behaviour were entirely a matter of course.)

"If you want to know," Törless replied, in embarrassment, "I think he's a low skunk."

"Isn't he just? A thorough skunk."

"But you're going in for something a bit off-colour yourself!" And Törless smiled in a rather forced manner, for he was ashamed of not being more indignant with Reiting.

"Me?" Reiting shrugged his shoulders. "What harm does it do? One's got to have had all sorts of experiences, and if *he*'s stupid and low enough . . ."

"Have you talked to him since?" Beineberg now interposed.

"Yes. He came to me yesterday evening, asking for money, because he's got into debt again and can't pay up."

"Did you give him any?"

"No, not yet."

"Excellent," Beineberg commented. "Then we've got just the opportunity we want for settling his hash. You might tell him to come along somewhere tonight."

"Where? The cubby-hole?"

"No, I don't think so. He doesn't need to know about that yet. But make him come up to the attic where you took him before."

"What time?"

"Let's say—eleven."

"Right.—D'you want to come for a bit of a walk now?"

"Yes. I expect Törless still has lots to do—haven't you, Törless?"

He actually had no more work to do, but he could feel that the other two were up to something together that they wanted to keep a secret from him. He was annoyed with himself for being too stiff to push his way in whether they wanted him or not.

So he watched them go, jealously, and racked his brains about what they might be planning in secret.

And as he watched them it struck him how much innocent grace and charm there was in Reiting's erect carriage and supple walk—just as there was in his way of talking. By contrast he tried to imagine what Reiting must have been like—inwardly, in his emotions—that other night. It must have been like some long, slow sinking of two souls with a mortal stranglehold on each other, and then depths as of some subterranean realm—

95

and, in between, a moment in which the sounds of the world, far, far above, faded and died out.

Could a human being really be so gay and easy-going again after such an experience ? Surely then it could not mean so much to him. Törless would have liked to ask him. And instead of that, now, in his childish timidity, he had left him with that spidery creature Beineberg !

At a quarter to eleven Törless saw Beineberg and Reiting slip out of their beds, and he also got up and began dressing.

"Ssh! I say, wait, can't you? Somebody'll notice if the three of us all go out together."

Törless got back under the bed-clothes.

A little while later they all met in the passage, and with their usual caution they went on upstairs to the attics.

"Where's Basini?" Törless asked.

"He's coming up the other way. Reiting gave him the key."

They went all the way in darkness. Only when they reached the top, outside the big iron door, did Beineberg light his little hurricane-lamp.

The lock was stiff. It was rusty from years of disuse and would not answer to the skeleton key. Then at last it gave, with a loud snap. The heavy door scraped back reluctantly on its rusty hinges, yielding only inch by inch.

From inside the attic came a breath of warm, stale air, like that in small hothouses.

Beineberg shut the door after them.

They went down the little wooden staircase and then squatted on the floor beside a huge roof-beam.

On one side of them were some large water-tubs for use in case of fire. It was obvious that the water in them had not been changed for a very long time; it had a sweet, sickly smell.

The whole place was oppressive, with the hot, bad air under the roof and the criss-cross pattern of the huge beams and rafters, some of them vanishing into the darkness overhead, some of them reaching down to the floor, forming a ghostly network.

Beineberg shaded his lamp, and there they sat quite still in the dark, not speaking a word—for long, long minutes.

Then the door in the darkness at the other end of the attic creaked, faintly, hesitantly. It was a sound to make one's heart leap into one's mouth—the first sound of the approaching prey.

Then came some unsure footsteps, a foot stumbling against wood, a dull sound as of a falling body . . . Silence . . . Then again hesitant footsteps . . . A pause . . . A faint voice asking: " Reiting ? "

Now Beineberg removed the shade from his lamp, throwing a broad ray of light in the direction from which the voice had come.

Several immense wooden beams loomed up, casting deep shadows. Apart from that, there was nothing to be seen but the cone of light with dust whirling in it.

The footsteps grew steadier and came closer.

Then—and this time quite near—a foot banged against wood again, and the next moment—framed in the wide base of the cone of light—Basini's face appeared, ash-grey in that uncertain illumination.

*　　*　　*

Basini was smiling—sweetly, cloyingly. It was like the fixed smile of a portrait, hanging above them there in the frame of light.

Törless sat still, pressing himself tightly against the woodwork ; he felt his eyelids twitching.

98

Now Beineberg recited the list of Basini's infamies—monotonously, in a hoarse voice.

Then came the question : " So you're not ashamed at all ? " At that Basini looked at Reiting, and his glance seemed to say : ' Now I think it's time for you to help me.' And at that moment Reiting hit him in the face so that he staggered back, tripped over a beam, and fell. Beineberg and Reiting leapt upon him.

The lamp had been kicked sideways, and now its light flowed senselessly, idly, past Törless's feet, across the floor. . . .

From the sounds in the darkness Törless could tell that they were pulling Basini's clothes off and then that they were whipping him with something thin and pliant. Evidently they had had everything prepared. He heard Basini's whimpering and half-stifled cries of pain as he went on pleading for mercy ; and then finally he heard nothing but a groaning, a suppressed howling, and at the same time Beineberg cursing in a low voice and his heavy, excited breathing.

Törless had not stirred from where he sat. Right at the beginning, indeed, he had been seized with a savage desire to leap up too and join in the beating ; but his feeling that he would come too late and only be one too many had held him back. His limbs were encased in paralysing rigidity, as though in the grip of some great hand.

In apparent indifference he sat staring at the floor. He did not strain his ears to distinguish what the various sounds meant, and his heart beat no faster than usual. His eyes followed the light that spread out in a pool at his feet. Grains of dust gleamed in it, and one ugly little cobweb. And the light seeped further, into the darkness under the beams, and petered out in dusty, murky gloom.

Törless could have sat there like that for an hour

without noticing the passing of time. He was thinking of nothing, and yet he was inwardly very much preoccupied. At the same time he was observing himself. And it was like gazing into a void and there seeing himself as if out of the corner of his eye, in a vague, shapeless glimmer. And then out of this vagueness—as though coming round the corner of his mind—slowly, but ever more distinctly, a desire advanced into clear consciousness.

Something made Törless smile at this. Then once again the desire came more strongly, trying to draw him from his squatting position down on to his knees, on to the floor. It was an urge to press his body flat against the floorboards ; and even now he could feel how his eyes would grow larger, like a fish's eyes, and how through the flesh and bones of his body his heart would slam against the wood.

Now there was indeed a wild excitement raging in Törless, and he had to hold on tight to the beam beside him in an effort to fight off the dizziness that was trying to draw him downwards.

Sweat pearled on his forehead, and he wondered anxiously what all this could mean.

Startled quite out of his former indifference, he was now straining his ears again to hear what the other three were doing in the darkness.

It had grown quiet over there. Only Basini could be heard groping for his clothes and moaning softly to himself.

An agreeable sensation went through Törless when he heard this whimpering. A tickling shudder, like thin spidery legs, ran up and down his spine, then contracted between his shoulder blades, pulling his scalp tight as though with faint claws. He was disconcerted to realise that he was in a state of sexual excitement. He thought back, and though he could not remember when this had begun, he knew it had already been there when he felt that peculiar desire to press himself against the floor. He was ashamed of it; but it was like a tremendous surge of blood going through him, numbing his thoughts.

Beineberg and Reiting came groping their way back and sat down in silence beside him. Beineberg looked at the lamp.

At this moment Törless again felt drawn downward. It was something that came from his eyes—he could feel that now—a sort of hypnotic rigidity spreading from the eyes to the brain. It was a question, indeed, it was—no, it was a desperation—oh, it was something he knew already—the wall, that garden outside the window, the low-ceilinged cottages, that childhood memory—it was all the same thing! all the same! He glanced at Beineberg. 'Doesn't he feel anything?' he wondered. But Beineberg was bending down, about to put the lamp straight. Törless gripped his arm to stop him.

"Isn't it like an eye?" he said, pointing to the light streaming across the floor.

"Getting poetical now, are you?"

"No. But don't you yourself say there's something special about eyes? It's all in your own favourite ideas about hypnotism—how sometimes they send out a force different from anything we hear about in physics. And it's a fact you can often tell far more about someone from his eyes than from what he says . . ."

"Well—what of it?"

"This light seems like an eye to me—looking into a strange world. It makes me feel as if I had to guess something. Only I can't. I only could gulp it down—drink it."

"Well, so you really are getting poetical."

"No, I'm perfectly serious. It simply makes me frantic. Just look at it yourself and you'll see what I mean. It makes you sort of want to wallow in the pool of it—to crawl right into that dusty corner on all fours, as if that were the way to guess it . . ."

" My dear chap, these are idle fancies, all nonsense. That'll be enough of that sort of thing for the moment."

Beineberg now bent right down and restored the lamp to its former position. But Törless felt a sudden spiteful satisfaction. He realised that, with some extra faculty he had, he got more out of these happenings than his companions did.

He was now waiting for Basini to re-appear, and with a secret shudder he noticed that his scalp was again tightening under those faint claws.

After all, he knew quite well by now that there was something in store for him, and the premonition of it was coming to him at ever shorter intervals, again and again : it was a sensation of which the others knew nothing, but which must evidently be of great importance for his future life.

Only he did not know what could be the meaning of this sexual excitement that was mingled with it. He did remember, however, that it had in fact been present each time when things began to be queer—though only to him —and to torture him because he could find no reason for the queerness.

And he resolved that at the next opportunity he would think hard about this. For the moment he gave himself up entirely to the shudder of excitement with which he looked for Basini's re-appearance.

Since Beineberg had replaced the lamp, the rays of light once again cut out a circle in the darkness, like an empty frame.

And all at once there was Basini's face again, just as it had been the first time, with the same fixed, sweet, cloying smile—as though nothing had happened in the meantime—only now, over his upper lip, mouth, and chin, slowly, drops of blood were making a red, wriggling line, like a worm.

*　*　*

" Sit down over there ! " Reiting ordered, pointing to the great beam. When Basini had obeyed, Reiting launched out : " I suppose you were thinking you'd got yourself nicely out of the whole thing, eh ?　I suppose you thought I was going to help you ?　Well, that's just where you were wrong.　What I've been doing with you was only to see exactly *how* much of a skunk you are."

Basini made a gesture of protest, at which Reiting moved as though to leap at him again.　Then Basini said : " But look, for heaven's sake, there wasn't anything else I could do ! "

" Shut up ! "　Reiting barked at him.　" We're sick and tired of your excuses !　We know now, once and for all, just where we stand with you, and we shall act accordingly."

There was a brief silence.　Then suddenly Törless said quietly, almost amiably : " Come on, say 'I'm a thief'."

Basini stared at him with wide, startled eyes.　Beineberg laughed approvingly.

But Basini said nothing.　Then Beineberg hit him in the ribs and ordered sharply : " Can't you hear ? You've been told to say you're a thief.　Get on and *say* it ! "

Once again there was a short, scarcely perceptible pause.　Then in a low voice, in a single breath, and with as little expression as possible, Basini murmured : " I'm a thief."

Beineberg and Reiting laughed delightedly, turning to Törless : " That was a good idea of yours, laddie."

And then to Basini : " And now get on with it and say :
I'm a beast, a pilfering, dishonest beast, *your* pilfering, dishonest, filthy beast."

And Basini said it, all in one breath, with his eyes shut.

But Törless had leaned back into the darkness again.
The scene sickened him, and he was ashamed of having
delivered up his idea to the others.

DURING the mathematics period Törless was suddenly struck by an idea.

For some days past he had been following lessons with special interest, thinking to himself : 'If this is really supposed to be preparation for life, as they say, it must surely contain some clue to what I am looking for, too.'

It was actually of mathematics that he had been thinking, and this even before he had had those thoughts about infinity.

And now, right in the middle of the lesson, it had shot into his head with searing intensity. As soon as the class was dismissed he sat down beside Beineberg, who was the only person he could talk to about such things.

"I say, did you really understand all that stuff?"

"What stuff?"

"All that about imaginary numbers."

"Yes. It's not particularly difficult, is it? All you have to do is remember that the square root of minus one is the basic unit you work with."

"But that's just it. I mean, there's no such thing. The square of every number, whether it's positive or negative, produces a positive quantity. So there *can't* be any real number that could be the square root of a minus quantity."

"Quite so. But why shouldn't one try to perform the operation of working out the square root of a minus quantity, all the same? Of course it can't produce any real value, and so that's why one calls the result an imaginary one. It's as though one were to say : someone always used to sit here, so let's put a chair ready for him today too, and even if he has died in the meantime, we shall go on behaving as if he were coming."

" But how can you when you know with certainty, with mathematical certainty, that it's impossible ? "

" Well, you just go on behaving as if it weren't so, in spite of everything. It'll probably produce some sort of result. And after all, where is this so different from irrational numbers—division that is never finished, a fraction of which the value will never, never, never be finally arrived at, no matter how long you may go on calculating away at it ? And what can you imagine from being told that parallel lines intersect at infinity ? It seems to me if one were to be over-conscientious there wouldn't be any such thing as mathematics at all."

" You're quite right about that. If one pictures it that way, it's queer enough. But what is actually so odd is that you *can really* go through quite ordinary operations with imaginary or other impossible quantities, all the same, and come out at the end with a tangible result ! "

" Well, yes, the imaginary factors must cancel each other out in the course of the operation just so that does happen."

" Yes, yes, I know all that just as well as you do. But isn't there still something very odd indeed about the whole thing ? I don't quite know how to put it. Look, think of it like this : in a calculation like that you begin with ordinary solid numbers, representing measures of length or weight or something else that's quite tangible —at any rate, they're real numbers. And at the end you have real numbers. But these two lots of real numbers are connected by something that simply doesn't exist. Isn't that like a bridge where the piles are there only at the beginning and at the end, with none in the middle, and yet one crosses it just as surely and safely as if the whole of it were there? That sort of operation makes me feel a bit giddy, as if it led part of the way God knows where. But what I really feel is so uncanny is the force that lies in a problem like that, which keeps such a firm hold on you that in the end you land safely on the other side."

Beineberg grinned. "You're starting to talk almost like the chaplain, aren't you? You see an apple—that's light-waves and the eye and so forth—and you stretch out your hand to steal it—that's the muscles and the nerves that set them in action—but between these two there lies something else that produces one out of the other, and that is the immortal soul, which in doing so has committed a sin . . . ah yes, indeed, none of your actions can be explained without the soul, which plays upon you as upon the keys of a piano . . ." And he imitated the cadences in which the chaplain was in the habit of producing this old simile. "Not that I find all that stuff particularly interesting."

"I thought you were the very person who would find it interesting. Anyway, it made me think of you at once because—if it's really impossible to explain it—it almost amounts to a piece of evidence for what you believe."

"Why shouldn't it be impossible to explain? I'm inclined to think it's quite likely that in this case the inventors of mathematics have tripped over their own feet. Why, after all, shouldn't something that lies beyond the limits of our intellect have played a little joke on the intellect? But I'm not going to rack my brains about it: these things never get anyone anywhere."

THAT same day Törless asked the mathematics master for permission to call on him, in order to discuss some points in the last lesson.

The next day, during the noon break, he went upstairs to the master's little apartment.

He had gained an entirely new respect for mathematics, for now it seemed all of a sudden to have ceased to be a dead school subject and to have turned into something very much alive. And arising out of this respect he felt something like envy of the master, who must be on familiar terms with all these processes and relationships and who carried the knowledge of them about with him always, like the key to a locked garden. But above and beyond this Törless was also impelled by curiosity, though it was, to be sure, rather diffident curiosity. He had never before been in the room of a grown-up young man, and there was a certain titillation in wondering what things looked like in the life of such a person, a different person, one who knew things and yet was composed and calm, at least so far as one could tell from the external objects surrounding him.

He had always been shy and withdrawn in his relations with his teachers and believed that as a result he was not particularly well liked by them. Hence his request, as he now paused in agitation outside the door, seemed to him an act of daring in which the main object was less to get some further light on his difficulties—for at the back of his mind he had already begun to doubt that he would get any—than to cast a glance, as it were, past the master and into this man's daily cohabitation with mathematics.

He was shown into the study. It was a long narrow room with a single window; near the window was a desk spattered with ink-blots, and against the wall was a sofa covered in some scratchy green ribbed material, with tassels. Over this sofa a faded student's cap hung on the wall, together with a number of photographs, the size of visiting-cards, brown and now grown dark with age, dating from the master's university days. On the oval table with the knock-kneed legs, which were of a would-be grace and prettiness that had somehow gone wrong, there lay a pipe and some leafy, crude-cut tobacco. The whole room was permeated with the smell of cheap tobacco-smoke.

Törless had scarcely had time to make these observations and note a trace of discomfort in himself, as on contact with something unsavoury, when the master came in.

He was a fair, nervous young man of no more than thirty, and quite a sound mathematician, who had already submitted several important papers to the academy.

He at once sat down at his desk, rummaged about a little among the papers strewn upon it (later it struck Törless that he had positively taken refuge there), then, crossing his legs, he began to polish his *pince-nez* with his handkerchief, and fixed an expectant gaze on Törless.

Meanwhile Törless had been scrutinising him too. He observed a pair of thick white woollen socks and saw that over them the bands of the underpants had been rubbed black by the blacking on the boots.

In contrast the handkerchief peeping out of the breast pocket was all white and dainty, and though the tie was a made-up one, it counterbalanced this by being as magnificently gaudy as a painter's palette.

Törless could not help feeling further repelled by these little observations; he scarcely found it in him to go on hoping that this man was really in possession of significant knowledge, when there was nothing whatsoever about either his person or his surroundings to suggest that it might be so. He had been secretly imagining a mathematician's study quite differently and as somehow expressive of the awe-inspiring matters that were excogitated there. The ordinariness of what he saw affronted him; he projected this on to mathematics, and his respect began to give way before a mistrustful reluctance.

And since the master was now shifting impatiently on his chair, not knowing what to make of this long silence and this scrutinising gaze, even at this stage there was already an atmosphere of misunderstanding between the two people in the room.

"And now let us . . . now you . . . I shall be pleased to tell you whatever you want to know," the master began at last.

Törless then came out with his difficulties, exerting himself to make clear what they meant to him. But he felt as though he were talking through a dense and gloomy fog, and his best words died away in his throat.

The master smiled, now and then gave a little fidgety cough, said: "If you don't mind," and lit a cigarette, at which he took hasty puffs. The cigarette-paper—and this was yet another thing that Törless noticed and found incredibly sordid—at each puff became greasy and crumpled up, crackling a little. The master took off his *pince-nez*, put it on again, nodded . . . And finally he cut Törless short. "I am delighted, my dear Törless, yes, I am indeed delighted," he said, interrupting him, " your qualms are indications of a seriousness and a readiness to think for yourself, of a . . . h'm . . . but it is not at all easy to give you the explanation you want. . . . Now, you must not misunderstand what I am going to say.

"It is like this, you see—you have been speaking of the intervention of transcendent, h'm, yes—of what are called *transcendent* factors. . . .

"Now of course I don't know what you feel about this. It's always a very delicate matter dealing with the suprasensual and all that lies beyond the strict limits of reason. I am not really qualified to intervene there in any way. It doesn't come into my field. One may hold this view or that, and I should greatly wish to avoid entering into any sort of controversy with anyone . . . But as regards mathematics," and he stressed the word 'mathematics' as though he were slamming some fateful door once and for all, " yes, as regards mathematics, we can be quite definite that here the relationships also work out in a natural and purely mathematical way.

" Only I should really—in order to be strictly scientific —I should really have to begin by posing certain preliminary hypotheses that you would scarcely grasp, at your stage. And apart from that, we have not the time.

" You know, I am quite prepared to admit that, for instance, these imaginary numbers, these quantities that have no real existence whatsoever, ha-ha, are no easy nut for a young student to crack. You must accept the fact that such mathematical concepts are nothing more or less than concepts inherent in the nature of purely mathematical thought. You must bear in mind that to anyone at the elementary stage at which you still are it is very difficult to give the right explanation of many things that have to be touched upon. Fortunately, very few boys at your stage feel this, but if one does really come along, as you have today—and of course, as I said before, I am delighted—really all one can say is : My dear young friend, you must simply take it on trust. Some day, when you know ten times as much mathematics as you do today, you will understand—but for the present : believe !

" There is nothing else for it, my dear Törless. Mathematics is a whole world in itself and one has to have lived in it for quite a while in order to feel all that essentially pertains to it."

Törless was glad when the master stopped talking. Since he had heard that door slam it had seemed to him that the words were moving farther and farther away from him . . . towards that other, indifferent realm where all correct and yet utterly irrelevant explanations lie.

But he was dazed by the torrent of words and the failure, and did not instantly grasp the fact that now he should get up and go.

So, in order to put an end to it once and for all, the master looked for one last, convincing argument.

On a little table lay a volume of Kant, the sort of volume that lies about for the sake of appearances. This the master took up and held out to Törless.

" You see this book. Here is philosophy. It treats of the grounds determining our actions. And if you could fathom this, if you could feel your way into the depths of this, you would come up against nothing but just such principles, which are inherent in the nature of thought and do in fact determine everything, although they themselves cannot be understood immediately and without more ado. It is very similar to the case with mathematics. And nevertheless we continually act on these principles. There you have the proof of how important these things are. But," he said, smiling, as he saw Törless actually opening the book and turning the pages, " that is something you may well leave on one side for the present. I only wanted to give you an example which you may remember some day, later on. For the present I think it would still be a little beyond you."

ALL the rest of that day Törless was in a state of inward upheaval.

The fact that he had had the volume of Kant in his hand—this quite haphazard circumstance, to which he had paid little attention at the time—now worked mightily within him. The name of Kant was familiar enough to him, though only as a name, and its currency value for him was that which it had generally among those who even remotely occupied themselves with things of the mind—it was the last word in philosophy. And this authority it had was indeed part of the reason why Törless had hitherto spent so little time on serious reading.

For very young people, once they have got over the stage of wanting to be cab-drivers, gardeners or confectioners when they grow up, in their imaginings are inclined to set their ambitions for life in whatever field seems to hold out most chance for them to distinguish themselves. If they say they want to be doctors, it is sure to be because some time, somewhere, they have seen a well-furnished waiting-room crowded with patients, or a glass case containing mysterious and alarming surgical instruments, or the like; if they dream of a diplomatic career, it is because they are thinking of the urbane glamour of cosmopolitan drawing-rooms; in short, they choose their occupation according to the milieu in which they would most like to see themselves, and according to the pose in which they like themselves best.

Now, in Törless's hearing the name Kant had never been uttered except in passing and then in the tone in which one refers to some awe-inspiring holy man. And Törless could not think anything but that with Kant the problems of philosophy had been finally solved, so that since then it had become futile for anyone to concern himself with the subject, just as he also believed there was no longer any point in writing poetry since Schiller and Goethe.

At home these men's works were kept in the book-case with the green glass panes in Papa's study, and Törless knew this book-case was never opened except to display its contents to a visitor. It was like the shrine of some divinity to which one does not readily draw nigh and which one venerates only because one is glad that thanks to its existence there are certain things one need no longer bother about.

This distorted relationship to philosophy and liter-ature in due course had its unhappy effect on Törless's development, and to it he owed many of these miserable hours. For in this way his ambition was diverted from the subjects to which he was really most inclined ; and while, being deprived of his natural goal, he was search-ing for another, his ambition fell under the coarse and resolute influence of his companions at school. His inclinations re-asserted themselves only occasionally and shamefacedly, each time leaving him with a sense of having done something useless and ridiculous. Never-theless they were so strong that he did not succeed in getting rid of them entirely ; and it was this unceasing conflict that left his personality without firm lines, with-out straightforward drive.

Today, however, this relationship seemed to have entered a new phase. The thoughts that had just caused him to seek in vain for enlightenment were no longer the baseless concatenations produced by the random play of his fantasy; on the contrary, they created upheaval in him, holding him in their grip, and with his whole body he could feel that behind them there pulsed an element of his life. This was something quite new for him. There was within him now something definite, a certainty that he had never known in himself before. It was someting mysterious, almost like a dream. It must, he thought to himself, have been very quietly developing under the various influences he had been exposed to in these last weeks, and now suddenly it was like imperious knuckles rapping at a door within him. His mood was that of a woman who for the first time feels the assertive stirring of the growing child within her.

He spent an afternoon full of wonderful enjoyment. He got out of his locker all the poetical scribblings that he had stored away there. Taking them with him, he sat down by the stove, where he remained quite alone and unseen behind the huge screen. He went through one copy-book after another, afterwards slowly tearing each into small shreds and throwing the pieces into the fire one by one, each time relishing the exquisite pathos of farewell.

In this way he meant to cast away all the impedimenta he had brought with him from earlier days, just as though he must now travel light, giving all his attention to the steps that had to be taken, on into the future.

At last he got up and went to join the others. He felt free, able to look at everything squarely. What he had done had actually been done only in a quite instinctive way; there was no surety that he would really be capable of being a new person now, none at all unless the sheer existence of that impulse was surety. 'Tomorrow,' he said to himself, 'tomorrow I shall go over everything very carefully, and I shall get a clear view of things all right somehow.'

He strolled about the room, between the separate desks, glanced into copy-books lying open, at the fingers moving swiftly and busily along in the act of writing on that glaring white paper, each finger drawing along after it its own little brown shadow—he watched all this like someone who had suddenly waked up, with eyes for which everything seemed now to be of graver import.

BUT the very next day brought a bad disappointment. What happened was that first thing in the morning Törless bought himself the cheap paper-bound edition of the book he had seen in his mathematics master's room, and made use of the first break between lessons to begin reading it. But with all its parentheses and foot-notes it was incomprehensible to him, and when he conscientiously went along the sentences with his eyes, it was as if some aged, bony hand were twisting and screwing his brain out of his head.

When after perhaps half an hour he stopped, exhausted, he had reached only the second page, and there was sweat on his forehead.

But then he clenched his teeth and read on, and he got to the end of one more page before the break was over.

That evening, however, he could not bring himself even to touch the book again. Was it dread ? Disgust ? He did not rightly know. Only one thing tormented him, with burning intensity : the mathematics master, that man who looked so thoroughly insignificant, quite openly had the book lying about in his room as if it were his daily entertainment.

He was in this mood when Beineberg came upon him.

" Well, Törless, how was it yesterday with the maths crammer ? " They were sitting alone in a window-bay and had pushed the long clothes-stand, on which all the coats hung, across in front of them, so that all they heard and saw of the class was the rising and falling hum of voices and the reflection of the lamps on the ceiling. Törless fiddled absent-mindedly with one of the coats hanging in front of him.

" I say, are you asleep ? He must have given you some answer, I suppose ? Though I must say I can imagine it got him in quite a fix, didn't it ? "

" Why ? "

" Well, I dare say he wasn't prepared for a silly question like that."

" It wasn't a silly question at all. I haven't done with it yet."

" Oh, I didn't mean it like that, I only meant it must have seemed silly to him. They learn their stuff off by heart just the way the chaplain can reel off the catechism, and if you go and ask them anything out of turn it always gets them in a fix."

" Oh, he wasn't at a loss for the answer. He didn't even let me finish saying what I wanted to say, he had it all so pat."

" And how did he explain the thing ? "

" Actually he didn't explain it at all. He said I wouldn't be able to understand it yet, these things were principles inherent in the mode of thought, and only become clear to someone who has gone on deeper into the subject."

" There you are, you see, there's the swindle of it ! They simply can't put their stuff across to someone who just has his brains and nothing else. It only works after he's spent ten years going through the mill. But up to then he's done thousands of calculations on the basis of the thing and erected huge constructions that always worked out to the last dot. What it means is he then simply believes in it the way a Catholic believes in revelation—it's always worked so nicely. And where's the difficulty, then afterwards, in getting such people to believe in the proof as well ? On the contrary, nobody would be capable of persuading them that though their construction stands, each single brick in it evaporates into thin air as soon as you try to get hold of it ! "

Beineberg's exaggeration made Törless feel uncomfortable.

" I don't think it's quite so bad as you make out. I've never doubted that mathematics is right—after all, the results show that it is—the only thing that seemed queer to me was that every now and then it all seems to go against reason. And after all it's quite possible that that only seems to be so."

" Well, you can wait and see at the end of ten years, and perhaps by then your brain will be properly softened up and receptive to it. But I've been thinking about it too since we talked the other day, and I'm perfectly convinced there's a catch in it somewhere. Come to think of it, you talked about it quite differently then from the way you're talking today."

" Oh no. It still seems pretty dubious to me even now, only I'm not going to rush off into exaggerations the way you do. It certainly *is* thoroughly queer. The idea of the irrational, the imaginary, the lines that are parallel and yet meet at infinity—in other words, they do meet *somewhere*—it all simply staggers me ! When I start thinking about it, I feel stunned, as though I'd been hit on the head." Törless leaned forward, right into the shadows, and his voice was low and husky. " Everything was all so clear and plain in my head before. But now it's as if my thoughts were like clouds, and when I come to these particular things, it's like a sort of gap you look through into an infinite, indefinable distance. Mathematics is probably right. But what is this thing in my head, and what about all the others ?

Don't they feel it at all? How does it look to all of them? Or doesn't it look like anything?"

"It seems to me you could see that from how your maths master reacted. When *you* hit on a thing like that, you always take a look round and wonder : now how does this fit in with everything else in me? *They've* bored a track through their brains, with thousands of spiral whorls in it, and they can only see as far as the last turning, whenever they look back to see if the thread they spin out behind them is still holding. That's why it gets them in a fix when you come along with that sort of question. None of *them* ever finds the way back. And anyway, how can you say I'm exaggerating? These people who've grown up and become so very clever have just spun themselves up completely in a web, with each mesh of it keeping the next in place, so that the whole thing looks as large as life and twice as natural. But there's nobody who knows where the first mesh is that keeps all the rest in place.

"The two of us have never talked seriously about this before—after all one doesn't particularly care to make a lot of fuss about such things—but now you can see for yourself what a feeble point of view these people have and how they come to terms with their world. It's all delusion, it's all swindle, mere feebleness of mind! It's anæmic! Their intellect takes them just far enough for them to think their scientific explanation out of their heads—but once it's outside it freezes up, see what I mean? Ha ha! All these fine points, these extreme fine points that the masters tell us are so fine and sharp that we're not capable of touching them yet —they're all dead—frozen—d'you see what I mean? There are these admired icy points sticking out in all directions, and there isn't anyone who can do anything with them, they're so dead!"

For some time now Törless had been leaning back again. Beineberg's hot breath was caught up among the coats and made the little corner warm. And as always when he was excited, Beineberg made a disagreeable impression on Törless. It was especially so now when he thrust up close, so close that his unwinking, staring eyes were like two greenish stones straight in front of Törless's own eyes, while his hands darted this way and that in the half-darkness with a peculiarly repellent nimbleness.

"Everything they assert is quite uncertain. They say everything works by a natural law. When a stone falls, that's the force of gravity. But why shouldn't it be the Will of God? And why should someone in whom God is well pleased not some time be liberated from sharing the fate of the stone? Still, why am I saying such things to you? You'll never be more than half a human being, anyway! Discovering a little bit of something queer, shaking your head a little, being horrified a little—that's your way. Beyond that you just don't dare to go. Not that it's any loss to me."

"But it is to me, you think? Yet it isn't as if your own statements were by any means so certain."

"How can you say such a thing! They're the only thing that *is* certain. Anyway, why should I quarrel with you about it? You'll see all right some day, my dear Törless. I'd even be prepared to bet that the day will come when you'll be quite confoundedly interested in the way it is with these things. For instance, when things with Basini turn out as I——"

"I don't want to hear about that," Törless cut him short. "I don't want that mixed up with it just now."

"Oh, and why not?"

"Just like that. I don't want to, that's all. I don't

care for it. Basini and this are two different things for me. This is one thing, and Basini is an entirely different kettle of fish."

Beineberg grimaced in annoyance at this unaccustomed decisiveness, indeed roughness, on the part of his younger friend. But Törless himself realised that the mere mention of Basini had undermined all the confidence he had been displaying, and in order to conceal this he talked himself into annoyance too.

"Anyway you make these sweeping statements with a certainty that's positively mad. Hasn't it occurred to you that your theories may be just as much without a solid basis as anyone else's? The spiral whorls in your own head go a lot deeper and call for a whole lot more good will."

Remarkably enough, Beineberg did not lose his temper. He only smiled—though rather twistedly, and his eyes gleamed more restlessly than ever—and he said over and over again : "You'll see for yourself, you'll see for yourself . . ."

"Well, what shall I see? Oh, all right then, I'll see, I'll see. But I don't give a damn about it, Beineberg ! It doesn't interest me. You don't understand me. You simply don't know what interests me. If mathematics torments me and if "—but he instantly thought better of it and said nothing about Basini—" if mathematics torments me, it's because I'm looking for something quite different behind it from what you're looking for. What I'm after isn't anything supernatural at all. It's precisely the natural—don't you see? nothing outside myself at all—it's something in me I'm looking for ! something natural, but, all the same, something I don't understand ! Only you have just as little feeling for it as any maths master in the world. Oh, leave me in peace—I've had enough of your speculations ! "

Törless was trembling with agitation when he stood up.

And Beineberg was saying over and over again: " Well, we shall see, we shall see . . ."

WHEN Törless was in bed that night he could not sleep. The quarters of the hours crept away like nurses tiptoeing from a sick-bed ; his feet were icy cold, and the blankets merely lay heavy on him without warming him.

In the dormitory there was nothing to be heard but the calm and regular breathing of the boys, all sunk in their healthy, animal sleep after their lessons, gymnastics, and running about in the open air.

Törless listened to the sleepers' breathing. There was Beineberg's, Reiting's, Basini's breathing—which was which ? He did not know. But each was one of the many regular, equally calm, equally steady sounds of breathing that rose and fell like the working of some mechanism.

One of the linen blinds had jammed half-way down, and under it the clear night shone into the room, marking out a pale, motionless rectangle on the floor. The cord must have got stuck at the top, or it had slipped off the roller, and now it hung down, hideously twisted, and its shadow crept like a worm across the bright rectangle on the floor.

It was all grotesquely, frighteningly hideous.

Törless tried to think of something pleasant. Beineberg came into his mind. Had he not taken him down a peg today ? Dealt a blow to his sense of superiority ? Had he today not succeeded for the first time in asserting his individuality against him ? In making it apparent in such a way that the other must have felt the infinite difference in the fineness of sensibility distinguishing their two views of things? Had there been anything left for Beineberg to say? Yes or no?

But this 'yes or no?' swelled up inside his head like a great bubble rising, and burst . . . and 'yes or no?' . . . 'yes or no?' . . . bubble after bubble rose and swelled, ceaselessly, in a stamping rhythm like the clatter of a railway train running over the rails, like the nodding of flowers on excessively long stems, like the thudding of a hammer that could be heard through many thin walls, in a silent house . . . This insistent, complacent 'yes or no?' disgusted Törless. His pleasure was not quite genuine, it hopped about so ridiculously.

And finally, when he started up, it seemed to be his own head that was nodding, lolling about on his shoulders, or thudding up and down like a hammer . . .

In the end all grew quiet in him. Before his eyes there was only a great circular plain spreading out in all directions.

Then . . . right from the very edge . . . there came two tiny, wobbling figures . . . tiny figures approaching obliquely across the table. Evidently they were his parents. But they were so small that he could not feel anything about them.

At the far rim they vanished again.

Then came another two—but look, there was somebody running up behind them and past them—with strides twice as long as his body—and an instant later he had vanished over the edge of the table. Had it not been Beineberg? Now for the two—wasn't one of them the mathematics master? Törless recognised him by the handkerchief coyly peeping out of his breast-pocket. But the other? The one with the very, very thick book under his arm, which was half as big as himself, so that he could only just manage to trudge along with it? . . .

At every third step they stopped and set the book down on the ground. And Törless heard his teacher say in a squeaky little voice : ' If that is really so, we shall find the right answer on page twelve, page twelve refers us then to page fifty-two, but then we must also bear in mind what is pointed out on page thirty-one, and on this supposition . . . ' As he spoke they were stooping over the book and plunging their hands into it, making the pages fly. After a while then they straightened up, and the other stroked the master's cheek five or six times. Then once more they went on a few paces, and after that Törless yet again heard the voice, just as if it were un-ravelling the long skein of some theorem in a mathematics lesson ; and this went on until the other again stroked the master's cheek.

This other . . . ? Törless frowned in the effort to see more clearly. Was he not wearing a peruke ? And rather old-fashioned clothes ? Very old-fashioned in-deed ? In fact, silk knee-breeches ? Wasn't it——? Oh ! And Törless woke up with a cry : " Kant ! "

The next moment he smiled. All was quiet around him ; the sleepers' breathing was very quiet now. He too had been asleep. And meanwhile his bed had grown warm. He stretched luxuriously under the bed-clothes.

' So I've been dreaming about Kant,' he thought to himself. ' Why didn't it last longer ? Perhaps he would have let me into some of the secret . . .' For he remembered that once recently when he had not done his history preparation he had all night long dreamt of the persons and events concerned, so vividly that the next day he had been able to recount it all just as though he had been there, and he had passed the test with distinction. And now he thought of Beineberg again, Beineberg and Kant—their discussion the previous day.

Slowly the dream receded—slowly, like a silk cover

slipping off the skin of a naked body, but without ever coming to an end.

Yet soon his smile faded again; he felt a queer uneasiness. Had he really come a single step forward in his thoughts? Could he really get anything, anything at all, out of this book that was supposed to contain the solution to all the riddles? And his victory? Oh, it was probably only his unexpected energy that had made Beineberg fall silent. . . .

And now again he was overwhelmed by profound discontent and a positively physical feeling of nausea. So he lay for long minutes, hollowed out by disgust.

But then again suddenly he became conscious of how his body was lapped by the mild, warm linen. Warily, quite slowly and warily, Törless turned his head. Sure enough, there the pale rectangle still lay on the floor— the sides of it now slanting rather differently, it was true, but still with that wormy shadow twisting across it. It was as if there some danger lay bound in chains, something that he could contemplate from here in his bed, as though protected by the bars of a cage, with the calm knowledge that he was in safety.

In his skin, all over his body, there awoke a sensation that suddenly turned into an image in his memory. When he was quite small—yes, yes, that was it—when he was still in pinafores and had not yet begun to go to kindergarten, there had been times when he had had a quite unspeakable longing to be a little girl. And this longing too had not been in his head—oh no—nor in his heart either—it had tingled all over his body and gone racing round under his skin. Yes, there had been moments when he so vividly felt himself a little girl that he believed it simply could not be otherwise. For at that time he still knew nothing of the significant bodily differences between the sexes, and did not understand why they all told him he must just put up with being a boy once and for all. And when he was asked why then he thought he would rather be a girl, he had not known how to say what he meant. . . .

Today for the first time he felt something similar again —again that longing, that tingling under the skin.

It was something that seemed to partake simultaneously of body and soul. It was a multifold racing and hurrying of something beating against his body, like the velvety antennae of butterflies. And mingled with it there was that defiance with which little girls run away when they feel that the grown-ups simply do not understand them, the arrogance with which they then giggle about the grown-ups, that timid arrogance which is always, as it were, poised for flight and which feels that at any instant it can withdraw into some terribly deep hiding-place inside its own little body. . . .

Törless laughed quietly to himself, and once again he stretched luxuriously under the bed-clothes.

How feverishly that quaint little mannikin he had dreamt of had gone leafing through the book ! And the rectangle down there on the floor ? Ha ha. Had such clever little mannikins ever in their lives noticed anything of that sort ? He felt vastly secure now, safe from those clever persons, and for the first time felt that in his sensuality—for he had long known that this was what it was—he had something that none of them could take away from him, and which none of them could imitate, either, something that was like a very high and very secret wall protecting him against all the cleverness of the outside world.

Had such clever little mannikins ever in their lives— he went on wondering—lain at the foot of a solitary wall and felt terror at every rustle inside the bricks and mortar, which was as though something dead were trying to find words that it might speak to them ? Had they ever felt the music that the breeze kindled among the autumn leaves, and felt it as he had—felt it through and through, so that suddenly there was terror looming behind it —terror that slowly, slowly turned into lust ? But into such strange lust, more like running away from something, and then like laughter and mockery. Oh, it is easy to be clever if one does not know all these questions. . . .

In the meantime, however, the mannikin every now and then grew to gigantic size, his face inexorably stern ; and each time this happened something like an electric shock ran agonisingly from Törless's brain all through his body. Then once again all his anguish at still being left to stand outside a locked door—the very thing that only an instant earlier had been flooded away by the warm waves of his pulsing blood—awoke in him again, and a wordless lament streamed through his spirit, like a dog's howling in the night, tremulous over an expanse of dark fields.

So he fell asleep. And even as he dropped off he looked across once or twice to the patch under the window, like someone mechanically reaching out for a supporting rope, to feel whether it is still taut. Then vaguely a resolution loomed up in his mind : the next day he would again do some hard thinking about himself . . . it would be best to do it with pen and paper . . . and then, last of all, there was only the pleasant warmth that lapped him . . . like a bath and a stirring of the senses . . . but no longer conscious to him as that, only in some utterly unrecognisable but very definite way being linked with Basini.

Then he slept soundly and dreamlessly.

AND yet this was the first thing in his mind when he woke the next morning. Now he intensely wished he could know what it had really been that he had half thought, half dreamt, about Basini as he fell asleep; but he could not manage to recollect it.

So all that remained was a tender mood such as reigns in a house at Christmas-time, when the children know the presents are already there, though locked away behind the mysterious door, and all that can be glimpsed now and then is a glow of light through the chinks.

In the evening Törless stayed in the class-room. Beineberg and Reiting had disappeared; probably they had gone off to the lair by the attics. Basini was sitting in his place in front, hunched over a book, his head supported on both hands.

Törless had bought himself a copy-book and now carefully set out his pen and ink. Then, after some hesitation, he wrote on the first page : De natura hominum. The Latin title was, he thought, the philosophic subject's due. Then he drew a large artistic curlicue round the title and leaned back in his chair to wait until it dried.

But it had been dry for a long time, and still he had not picked up his pen again. Something held him fast, kept him motionless. It was the hypnotic atmosphere of the big, hot lamps, and the animal warmth emanating from all the living bodies in the crowded room. He had always been susceptible to such an atmosphere, and this state was one that could rise to such a pitch of intensity that he became physically feverish, which again was always associated with an extraordinary heightening of mental perceptiveness. So it was today too. He had worked out, during the course of the day, what it actually was he wanted to make notes about : the whole series of those particular experiences from the evening with Božena on, culminating in that vague sensual state which had recently been coming over him. Once that was all put down, fact for fact, then—or so he hoped—the real intellectual pattern of it would emerge of its own accord, just as an encompassing line stands out distinctly and gives form to a tangled composition of hundreds of intersecting curves. And more than that he did not want. But so far he had fared like a fisherman who can feel by the jerking of his net that he has got a heavy haul and yet in spite of all his straining cannot manage to get it up into the light.

And now Törless did begin to write after all, but rapidly and without paying any attention to the form. " I feel something in me," he wrote, " and don't quite know what it is." Then, however, he hastily crossed this line out and wrote instead : " I must be ill—insane ! " At this a shudder went through him, for the word was pleasantly melodramatic. " Insane—else what is it that makes things seem so odd to me that are quite ordinary for the others ? And why does this oddness of things torment me ? And why does this oddness cause me lusts of the flesh ? "—he deliberately used this Biblical and unctuous expression because it struck him as more obscure and laden with implication. " Before, I used to have the same attitude to this as any of the others here——" but then he came to a halt. ' Is that really true ? ' he wondered. ' For instance, even that time at Božena's it was all so queer. So when did it actually begin ? . . . Oh well.' he thought, ' it doesn't matter. Some time, anyway.' But he left his sentence unfinished.

"What are the things that seem odd to me ? The most trivial. Mostly inanimate objects. What is it about them that seems odd ? Something about them that I don't know about. But that's just it ! Where on earth do I get this ' something ' notion from ? I feel it's there, it exists. It has an effect on me, just as if it were trying to speak. I get as frantic as a person trying to lip-read from the twisted mouth of someone who's paralysed, and simply not being able to do it. It's as if I had one extra sense, one more than the others have, but not completely developed, a sense that's there and makes itself noticed, but doesn't function. For me the world is full of soundless voices. Does this mean I'm a seer or that I have hallucinations ?

"But it's not only inanimate objects that have this effect on me. What makes me so much more doubtful about it all is that people do it too. Up to a certain point in time I saw them the way they see themselves. Beineberg and Reiting, for instance—they have their lair, a perfectly ordinary secret cubby-hole, because they enjoy having a place like that to retreat to. And they do one thing because they're furious with one fellow, they do another thing because they want to prevent someone else from having any influence on the others. All quite sensible, obvious reasons. But nowadays they sometimes appear to me as if I were having a dream and they were only people in it. It's not only what they say or what they do—everything about them, bound up with their physical presence, sometimes has the same sort of effect on me as inanimate objects have. And all the same, I still hear them talking exactly the same way as before, I see how what they do and say still follows the same old patterns . . . This really goes to show all the time that there's nothing extraordinary happening at all, and at the same time something in me still goes on protesting that it isn't like that. So far as I can remember exactly, this change began with Basini's——"

Here Törless involuntarily glanced over at Basini himself.

Basini was still sitting hunched over his book in the same attitude, apparently memorising something. At the sight of him sitting there like that, Törless's thoughts came to a standstill, and now he had a chance to feel once more the workings of the seductive torments that he had just been describing. For as soon as he became aware of how quietly and harmlessly Basini was sitting there before him, in no way differentiated from the others to right and to left, he vividly recalled the humiliations that Basini had undergone. They sprang to life in his mind : that is to say, he was far from thinking of them with the kind of indulgence which goes with the moral reflection that it is in every one's nature to try, after having suffered humiliations, to regain at least an outward air of casualness and unembarrassment as quickly as possible. On the contrary, something instantly began in him that was like the crazy whirling of a top, immediately compressing Basini's image into the most fantastically dislocated attitudes and then tearing it asunder in incredible distortions, so that he himself grew dizzy. True, these were only figures of speech that he found for it afterwards. At the moment he merely had the feeling of something in his tightened breast whirling upwards into his head, like a wildly spinning top, and this was the dizziness. Into the midst of it, like sparks, like dots of colour, there sprang those same feelings that he had had at various times about Basini.

Actually it had always been one and the same feeling. And more accurately, it was not a feeling at all, but more like a tremor deep down within him, causing no perceptible waves and nevertheless making his soul shudder quietly and yet so violently that in comparison the surges of even the stormiest feelings were like harmless ripples on the surface.

If this one ' feeling ' was one that had at different times seemed different to him, it was because all he had to help him in interpreting this tide of emotion that would flood through his whole being was the images it cast up into his consciousness—as if all that could be seen of a swell stretching endlessly far away into the darkness were single, separate droplets of foam flung high against the cliffs of some lighted shore and, all force spent, immediately falling away again, out of the circle of light.

So these impressions were unstable, varying, and accompanied by an awareness of their random nature. Törless could never hold on to them; and when he looked more closely, he could feel that these incidents on the surface were in no proportion to the force of the dark mass, deep down, of which they seemed to be the manifestations.

He never at any time ' saw ' Basini in any sort of physically plastic and living attitude; never did any of all this amount to a real vision. It was always only the illusion of one, as it were only the vision of his visions. For within him it was always as if a picture had just flashed across the mysterious screen, and he never succeeded in catching hold of it in the very instant that this happened. Hence there was all the time a restlessness and uneasiness in him such as one feels when watching cinematographic pictures, when, for all the illusion the whole thing creates, one is nevertheless unable to shake off a vague awareness that behind the image one perceives there are hundreds of other images flashing past, and each of them utterly different from the picture as a whole.

But he did not know where in himself to search for this power of creating illusion—illusion that was, moreover, by an immeasurably slight degree always just insufficient. He simply had an obscure inkling that it was connected with that enigmatic quality his spirit had of being assailed at times even by inanimate objects, by mere things, as by hundreds of mutely questioning eyes.

And so Törless sat quite still, transfixed, staring across at Basini, wholly involved in the seething whirl within him. And ever and again the same question rose up before him : What is this special quality I have ? Gradually he ceased to see Basini any longer, or the hot glaring lamps, ceased to feel the animal warmth surrounding him, or to hear the buzzing and humming that goes up from a crowd of human beings even if they are only whispering. It all merged into one hot, darkly glowing mass that swung in a circle round him. His ears were burning, and his finger-tips were icy cold. He was in that state of more psychic than bodily fever which he loved. The mood went on intensifying, and now and then impulses of tenderness mingled with it. Previously, when in this state, he had enjoyed abandoning himself to those memories that are left in a young soul when for the first time it has been touched by the warm breath of woman. And today too he felt that indolent warmth. A memory came to him . . . It was on a journey . . . in a little town in Italy . . . his parents and he were staying in a hotel not far from the theatre. Every evening the same opera was performed there, and every evening he heard every word and every note of it wafted over to him. He had no knowledge of the language ; but for all that he spent his evenings sitting at the open window, listening. So it came about that he fell in love with one of the singers, without ever having set eyes on her. He was never again so moved by the theatre as at that time ; the passion of those arias was for him like the wing-beats of great dark birds, and it was as though he could feel the lines that their flight traced in his soul. These were no longer human passions that he heard ; no, they were passions that had escaped out of the human hearts, taking flight as out of cages that were too cramped, too commonplace, for them. In that state of excitement he could never think of the people who were over there —invisible—acting out those passions. If he did try to picture them, on the instant dark flames shot up before his eyes—or undreamt-of gigantic dimensions opened up, as in the darkness people's bodies grow and people's eyes shine like the mirroring surface of deep wells. This lurid conflagration, these eyes in the dark, these black wing-beats, were what he at that time loved under the name of the singer he had never seen.

And who had composed the opera ? He did not know. Perhaps the libretto was some dreary sentimental romance. Had its creator ever felt that once set to music it would be transformed into something else ?

A sudden thought made his whole body grow tense. Are even older people like that ? Is the world like that ? Is it a universal law that there's something in us stronger, bigger, more beautiful, more passionate and darker than ourselves ? Something we have so little power over that all we can do is aimlessly strew thousands of seeds, until suddenly out of one seed it shoots up like a dark flame and grows away out over our heads ? . . . And every nerve in his body quivered with the impatient answer : Yes.

Törless glanced about him with blazing eyes. It was all still there, the lamps, warmth, and light, the boys busily at work. But here in the midst of it he seemed to himself as one elect—like a saint, having heavenly visions. For the intuition of great artists was something of which he did not know.

Hurriedly, with the hastiness of nervous dread, he snatched up his pen and made some notes on his discovery. Once again there seemed to be a light within him scattering its sparks in all directions . . . . then an ash-grey shower of rain fell over his gaze, and the glory in his spirit was quenched.

THE Kant episode was now practically over and done with. By day Törless had quite ceased to think of it; the conviction that he himself was very close to the answer to his riddles was much too strong for him to go on bothering about anyone else's way of dealing with such problems. Since the last evening it was as if he had already felt in his hand the knob of the door that would open into the further realm, and then it had slipped from his grasp. But since he had realised that he must manage without the aid of philosophic books, and since he put no real trust in them anyway, he was rather at a loss as to how he was to find that knob again. He several times made an attempt to continue his notes; but the written words remained lifeless, a series, it seemed, of irksome and all too familiar question-marks, and there was no re-awakening of that moment in which he had gazed through them as into a vault illumined by flickering candle-flames.

Therefore he resolved that as often as possible, and ever and again, he would seek those situations which had that for him so peculiar meaning. And especially often did his gaze rest on Basini, when the latter, having no sense of being watched, went about among the others as if nothing at all were wrong. 'Sooner or later,' Törless thought to himself, 'it'll come to life again, and then perhaps more intensely and clearly than before.' And he was quite relieved at the thought that where such things were concerned one was simply in a dark room and there was nothing else one could do, once the fingers had slipped from the right place, but keep on groping and groping at random over the walls in the dark.

Yet at night this thought lost some of its conviction, and he would be overtaken by something like shame at having shied away from his original resolve to seek in the book his teacher had shown him the explanation that it might, after all, contain. This happened when he was lying still and listening for the sound of breathing from Basini, whose outraged body drew breath as tranquilly as those of all the others. He would lie still like a stalker in his hiding-place, with the feeling that he only had to wait and the time so spent would surely bring its reward. And then the thought of the book would come into his mind, and at once a fine-toothed doubt would begin to gnaw in him, disturbing this stillness—a foreboding that he was wasting his time, a hesitant admission that he had suffered a defeat.

As soon as this vague feeling asserted itself, his attentiveness lost the comfortable quality of watching the development of a scientific experiment. It seemed then that some physical influence emanated from Basini, a fascination such as comes from sleeping near a woman and knowing one can at any instant pull the covers off her body. It was a tingling in the brain, which started from the awareness of only having to stretch out one's hand. It was the same thing that often drives young couples into orgies of sensuality far beyond the bodies' real demands.

* * *

According to the intensity with which it struck him that his enterprise would perhaps seem ridiculous even to himself if he knew all that Kant knew, all that his mathematics master knew, and all that those people knew who had got to the end of their studies—according to the varying force of this qualm in him there was a weakening or an intensification of those sensual impulses that often kept his burning eyes wide open, in spite of the stillness all round him, where everyone else was asleep. At times, indeed, these impulses overwhelmed all other thoughts. When at such moments he abandoned himself, half willingly, half despairingly, to their insinuations, it was with him only as it is with all those people who, after all, never so much incline to a mad outburst of soul-rending, wantonly destructive debauchery as when they have suffered some failure that upsets the balance of their self-confidence. . . .

Then, when at last, after midnight, he was drifting into an uneasy sleep, it several times seemed to him that someone got up, over where Reiting's and Beineberg's beds were, and took his coat and went across to Basini. Then they left the dormitory . . . But it might equally well have been imagination. . . .

THERE came two public holidays; and since they fell on a Monday and Tuesday, the headmaster gave the boys Saturday off as well, so that they had four days free. For Törless this was still too short a time to make the long journey home worth while; and he had therefore hoped that at any rate his parents would come and see him. However, his father was kept by urgent affairs at his government office, and his mother did not feel well enough to face the strain of travelling alone.

But when Törless received his parents' letter, in which they told him they could not come and added many affectionate words of comfort, he suddenly realised that this actually suited him very well. He knew now that it would have been almost an interruption—at least it would have embarrassed him considerably—if he had had to face his parents just at this stage.

Many of the boys had invitations to estates in the district. Dschjusch, whose parents owned a fine property at the distance of a day's drive from the little town, was one of those who went away, and with him went Beineberg, Reiting, and Hofmeier. Basini had also been asked, but Reiting had bidden him refuse. Törless excused himself on the grounds that he did not know for certain whether his parents might not come after all; he felt totally disinclined for innocent, cheerful frolics and amusements.

By noon on Saturday the great building was silent and almost quite deserted.

When Törless walked through the empty corridors, they echoed from end to end. There was nobody to bother about him, for most of the masters had also gone away for a few days' shooting or the like. It was only at meals, which were now served in a small room next to the deserted refectory, that the few remaining boys saw each other. When they left the table they once more took their separate ways through the many corridors and class-rooms; it was as if the silence of the building had swallowed them up, and whatever life they led in these intervals seemed to be of no more interest to anyone than that of the spiders and centipedes in the cellars and attics.

Of Törless's class the only two left were himself and Basini, with the exception of a few boys in the sick-bay. When leaving, Reiting had exchanged a few words in private with Törless in the matter of Basini, for he was afraid that Basini might make use of the opportunity to seek protection from one of the masters; he had therefore impressed it on Törless to keep a sharp eye on him.

However, there was no need of that to concentrate Törless's attention on Basini.

Scarcely had the uproar faded away—the carriages driving to the door, the servants carrying valises, the boys joking and shouting good-bye to each other— when the consciousness of being alone with Basini took complete possession of Törless's mind.

It was after the first midday meal. Basini sat in his place in front, writing a letter. Törless had gone to a corner right at the back of the room and was trying to read.

It was for the first time again the volume of Kant, and the situation was just as he had pictured it: in front there sat Basini, at the back himself, holding Basini with his gaze, boring holes into him with his eyes. And it was like this that he wanted to read : penetrating deeper into Basini at the end of every page. That was how it must be ; in this way he must find the truth without losing grip on life, living, complicated, ambiguous life. . . .

But it would not work. This was what always happened when he had thought something out all too carefully in advance. It was too unspontaneous, and his mood swiftly lapsed into a dense, gluey boredom, which stuck odiously to every one of his all too deliberate attempts to get on with his reading.

In a fury, Törless threw the book on the floor. Basini looked round with a start, but at once turned away again and hurriedly went on writing.

So the hours crept on towards dusk. Törless sat there in a stupor. The only thing that struck clearly into his awareness—out of a muffled, buzzing, whirring state of generalised sensation—was the ticking of his pocket-watch. It was like a little tail wagging on the sluggish body of the creeping hours. The room became blurred . . . Surely Basini could no longer be writing . . . 'Aha, he probably doesn't dare to light a lamp,' Törless thought to himself. But was he still sitting over there in his place at all ? Törless had been gazing out into the bleak, twilit landscape and now had to accustom his eyes again to the darkness of the room. Oh yes, there he was. There, that motionless shadow, that would be Basini all right. And now he even heaved a sigh— once, twice. He hadn't gone to sleep, had he ?

A servant came in and lit the lamps. Basini started up and rubbed his eyes. Then he took a book out of his desk and began to apply himself to it.

Törless could hardly prevent himself from speaking to him, and in order to avoid that he hurried out of the room.

IN the night Törless was not far from falling upon Basini, such a murderous lust had awakened in him after the anguish of that senseless, stupefying day. By good fortune sleep overtook him just in time.

The next day passed. It brought nothing but the same bleak and barren quietness. The silence and suspense worked on Törless's overwrought nerves; the ceaseless strain on his attention consumed all his mental powers, so that he was incapable of framing any thought at all.

Disappointed, dissatisfied with himself to the point of the most extreme doubt, he felt utterly mangled. He went to bed early.

He had for a long time been lying in an uneasy, feverishly hot half-sleep when he heard Basini coming.

Lying motionless, with his eyes he followed the dark figure walking past the end of his bed. He heard the other undressing, and then the rustling of the blankets being pulled over the body.

He held his breath, but he could not manage to hear any more. Nevertheless he did not lose the feeling that Basini was not asleep either, but was straining to hear through the darkness, just like himself.

So the quarter-hours passed . . . hours passed. Only now and then the stillness was broken by the faint sound of the bodies stirring, each in its bed.

Törless was in a queer state that kept him awake. Yesterday it had been sensual pictures in his imagination that had made him feverish. Only right at the end had they taken a turn towards Basini, as it were rearing up under the inexorable hand of sleep, which then blotted them out; and it was precisely of this that he had the vaguest and most shadowy memory. But tonight it had from the very beginning been nothing other than an impelling urge to get up and go over to Basini. So long as he had had the feeling that Basini was awake and listening for whatever sounds he might make, it had been scarcely endurable; and now that Basini was apparently asleep, it was even worse, for there was a cruel excitement in the thought of falling upon the sleeper as upon a prey.

Törless could already feel the movements of rising up and getting out of bed twitching in all his muscles. But still he could not yet shake off his immobility.

'And what am I going to do, anyway, if I do go over to him?' he wondered, in his panic almost speaking the words aloud. And he had to admit to himself that the cruelty and lust in him had no real object. He would have been at a loss if he had now really set upon Basini. Surely he did not want to beat him? God forbid! Well then, in what way was his wild sensual excitement to get fulfilment from Basini? Instinctively he revolted at the thought of the various little vices that boys went in for. Expose himself to another person like that? Never!

But in the same measure as this revulsion grew the urge to go over to Basini also became stronger. Finally Törless was completely penetrated with the sense of how absurd such an act was, and yet a positively physical compulsion seemed to be drawing him out of bed as on a rope. And while his mind grew blank and he merely kept on telling himself, over and over again, that it would be best to go to sleep now if he could, he was mechanically rising up in the bed. Very slowly—and he could feel how the emotional urge was gaining, inch by inch, over the resistance in him—he began to sit up. First one arm moved . . . then he propped himself on one elbow, then pushed one knee out from under the bed-clothes . . . and then . . . suddenly he was racing, bare-foot, on tip-toe, over to Basini, and sat down on the edge of Basini's bed.

Basini was asleep.

He looked as if he were having pleasant dreams.

Törless was still not in control of his actions. For a moment he sat still, staring into the sleeper's face. Through his brain there jerked those short, ragged thoughts which do no more, it seems, than record what a situation is, those flashes of thought one has when losing one's balance, or falling from a height, or when some object is torn from one's grasp. And without knowing what he was doing he gripped Basini by the shoulder and shook him out of his sleep.

Basini stretched indolently a few times. Then he started up and gazed at Törless with sleepy, stupefied eyes.

A shock went through Törless. He was utterly con-fused ; now all at once he realised what he had done, and he did not know what he was to do next. He was frightfully ashamed. His heart thudded loudly. Words of explanation and excuse hovered on the tip of his tongue. He would ask Basini if he had any matches, if he could tell him the time . . .

Basini was still goggling at him with uncomprehending eyes.

Now, without having uttered a word, Törless withdrew his arm, now he slid off the bed and was about to creep back soundlessly into his own bed—and at this moment Basini seemed to grasp the situation and sat bolt upright.

Törless stopped irresolutely at the foot of the bed.

147

Basini glanced at him once more, questioningly, searchingly, and then got out of bed, slipped into coat and slippers and went padding off towards the door. And in a flash Torless became sure of what he had long suspected : that this had happened to Basini many times before.

In passing his bed, Törless took the key to the cubbyhole, which he had been keeping hidden under his pillow.

Basini walked straight on ahead of him, up to the attics. He seemed in the meantime to have become thoroughly familiar with the way that had once been kept so secret from him. He steadied the crate while Törless stepped down on to it, he cleared the scenery to one side, carefully, with gingerly movements, like a well-trained flunkey.

Törless unlocked the door, and they went in. With his back to Basini, he lit the little lamp.

When he turned round, Basini was standing there naked.

Involuntarily Törless fell back a step. The sudden sight of this naked snow-white body, with the red of the walls dark as blood behind it, dazzled and bewildered him. Basini was beautifully built ; his body, lacking almost any sign of male development, was of a chaste, slender willowyness, like that of a young girl. And Törless felt this nakedness lighting up in his nerves, like hot white flames. He could not shake off the spell of this beauty. He had never known before what beauty was. For what was art to him at his age, what—after all —did he know of that ? Up to a certain age, if one has grown up in the open air, art is simply unintelligible, a bore !

And here now it had come to him on the paths of sexuality . . . secretly, ambushing him . . . There was an infatuating warm exhalation coming from the bare skin, a soft, lecherous cajolery. And yet there was something about it that was so solemn and compelling as to make one almost clasp one's hands in awe.

But after the first shock Törless was as ashamed of the one reaction as of the other. 'It's a man, damn it!' The thought enraged him, and yet it seemed to him as though a girl could not be different.

In his shame he spoke hectoringly to Basini: "What on earth d'you think you're doing? Get back into your things this minute!"

Now it was Basini who seemed taken aback. Hesitantly, and without shifting his gaze from Törless, he picked up his coat from the floor.

"Sit down—there!" Törless ordered. Basini obeyed. Törless leaned against the wall, with his arms crossed behind his back.

"Why did you undress? What did you want of me?"

"Well, I thought . . ."

He paused hesitantly.

"What did you think?"

"The others . . ."

"What about the others?"

"Beineberg and Reiting . . ."

"What about Beineberg and Reiting? What did they do? You've got to tell me everything! That's what I want. See? Although I've heard about it from them, of course." At this clumsy lie Törless blushed.

Basini bit his lips.

"Well? Get on with it!"

"No, don't make me tell! Please don't make me! I'll do anything you want me to. But don't make me tell about it. . . . Oh, you have such a special way of tormenting me. . . !" Hatred, fear, and an imploring plea for mercy were all mingled in Basini's gaze.

Törless involuntarily modified his attitude. "I don't

149

want to torment you at all. I only mean to make you tell the whole truth yourself. Perhaps for your own good."

" But, look, I haven't done anything specially worth telling about."

" Oh, haven't you ? So why did you undress, then ? "

" That's what they wanted."

" And why did you do what they wanted ? So you're a coward, eh ? A miserable coward ? "

" No, I'm not a coward ! Don't say that ! "

" Shut up ! If you're afraid of being beaten by them, you might find being beaten by me was something to remember ! "

" But it's not the beatings they give me that I'm afraid of ! "

" Oh ? What is it then ? "

By now Törless was speaking calmly again. He was already annoyed at his crude threat. But it had escaped him involuntarily, solely because it seemed to him that Basini stood up to him more than to the others.

" Well, if you're not afraid, as you say, what's the matter with you ? "

" They say if I do whatever they tell me to, after some time I shall be forgiven everything."

" By the two of them ? "

" No, altogether."

" How can they promise that ? *I* have to be considered too ! "

" They say they'll manage that all right."

This gave Törless a shock. Beineberg's words about Reiting's dealing with him, if he got the chance, in exactly the same way as with Basini now came back to him. And if it really came to a plot against him, how was he to cope with it ? He was no match for the two of them in that sort of thing. How far would they go ? The same as with Basini ? . . . Everything in him revolted at the perfidious idea.

Minutes passed between him and Basini. He knew that he lacked the daring and endurance necessary for such intrigues, though of course only because he was too little interested in that sort of thing, only because he never felt his whole personality involved. He had always had more to lose than to gain there. But if it should ever happen to be the other way, there would, he felt, be quite a different kind of toughness and courage in him. Only one must know when it was time to stake everything.

"Did they say anything more about it—how they think they can do it ? I mean, that about me."

"More ? No. They only said they'd see to it all right."

And yet . . . there was danger now . . . somewhere lying in wait . . . lying in ambush for Törless . . . every step could run him into a gin-trap, every night might be the last before the fight. There was tremendous insecurity in this thought. Here was no more idle drifting along, no more toying with enigmatic visions —this had hard corners and was tangible reality.

Törless spoke again :

"And what do they do with you ? "

Basini was silent.

"If you're serious about reforming, you have to tell me everything."

"They make me undress."

"Yes, yes, I see that for myself . . . And then ? "

A little time passed, and then suddenly Basini said : "Various things." He said it with an effeminate, coy expression.

"So you're their—mi—mistress ? "

"Oh no, I'm their friend ! "

"How can you have the nerve to say that ! "

" They say so themselves."

" What ! "

" Yes, Reiting does."

" Oh, Reiting does ? "

" Yes, he's very nice to me. Mostly I have to undress and read him something out of history-books—about Rome and the emperors, or the Borgias, or Timur Khan . . . oh well, you know, all that sort of big, bloody stuff. Then he's even affectionate to me. . . . And then afterwards he generally beats me."

" After what ? Oh, I see ! "

" Yes. He says, if he didn't beat me, he wouldn't be able to help thinking I was a man, and then he couldn't let himself be so soft and affectionate to me. But like that, he says, I'm his chattel, and so then he doesn't mind."

" And Beineberg ? "

" Oh, Beineberg's beastly. Don't you think too his breath smells bad ? "

" Shut up ! What I think is no business of yours ! Tell me what Beineberg does with you ! "

" Well, the same as Reiting, only . . . But you mustn't go yelling at me again. . . ."

" Get on with it."

" Only . . . he goes about it differently. First of all he gives me long talks about my soul. He says I've sullied it, but so to speak only the outermost forecourt of it. In relation to the innermost, he says, this is something that doesn't matter at all, it's only external. But one must kill it. In that way many people have stopped being sinners and become saints. So from a higher point of view sin isn't so bad, only one must carry it to the extreme, so that it breaks off of its own accord, he says. He makes me sit and stare into a prism. . . ."

" He hypnotises you ? "

" No, he says it's just that he must make all the things floating about on the surface of my soul go to sleep and become powerless. It's only then he can have intercourse with my soul itself."

" And how, may I ask, does he have intercourse with it ? "

" That's an experiment he hasn't ever brought off yet. He sits there, and I have to lie on the ground so that he can put his feet on me. I have to get quite dull and drowsy from staring into the glass. Then suddenly he orders me to bark. He tells me exactly how to do it—quietly, more whimpering—the way a dog whines in its sleep."

" What's that good for ? "

" Nobody knows what it's good for. And he also makes me grunt like a pig and keeps on and on telling me there's something of a pig about me, in me. But he doesn't mean it offensively, he just keeps on repeating it quite softly and nicely, in order—this is what he says —in order to imprint it firmly on my nerves. You see, he says it's possible one of my former lives was that of a pig and it must be lured out so as to render it harmless."

" And you believe all that stuff ? "

" Good lord, no ! I don't think he believes it himself. And then in the end he's always quite different, anyway. How on earth should I believe such things ? Who believes in a soul these days anyway ? And as for transmigration of souls——! I know quite well I slipped. But I've always hoped I'd be able to make up for it again. There isn't any hocus-pocus needed for that. Not that I spend any time racking my brains about how I ever came to go wrong. A thing like that comes on you so quickly, all by itself. It's only afterwards you notice that you've done something silly. But if he gets his fun out of looking for something supernatural behind it, let him, for all I care. For the present, after all, I've got to do what he wants. Only I wish he'd leave off sticking pins in me. . . ."

" What ? "

" Pricking me with a pin—not hard, you know, only just to see how I react—to see if something doesn't manifest itself at some point or other on the body. But it does *hurt*. The fact is, he says the doctors don't understand anything about it. I don't remember now how he proves all this, all I remember is he talks a lot about fakirs and how when they see their souls they're supposed to be insensitive to physical pain."

" Oh yes, I know those ideas. But you yourself say that's not all."

" No, it certainly isn't all. But I also said I think this is just a way of going about it. Afterwards there are always long times—as much as a quarter of an hour— when he doesn't say anything and I don't know what's going on in him. But after that he suddenly breaks out and demands services from me—as if he were possessed —much worse than Reiting."

" And you do everything that's demanded of you ? "

" What else can I do ? I want to become a decent person again and be left in peace."

" But whatever happens in the meantime won't matter to you at all ? "

" Well, I can't help it, can I ? "

" Now pay attention to me and answer my questions. How could you steal ? "

" How ? Look, it's like this, I needed money urgently. I was in debt to the tuck-shop man, and he wouldn't wait any longer. Then I really did believe there was money coming for me just at that time. None of the other fellows would lend me any. Some of them hadn't got any themselves, and the saving ones are always just glad if someone who isn't like that gets short towards the end of the month. Honestly, I didn't want to cheat anyone. I only wanted to borrow it secretly. . . ."

"That's not what I mean," Törless said impatiently, interrupting this story, which it was obviously a relief for Basini to tell. "What I'm asking is *how*—how were you able to do it, what did you feel like? What went on in you at that moment?"

"Oh well—nothing, really. After all, it was only a moment, I didn't feel anything, I didn't think about anything, simply it had suddenly happened."

"But the first time with Reiting? The first time he demanded those things of you? You know what I mean. . . ."

"Oh, I didn't like it, of course. Because it had to be done just like that, being ordered to. Otherwise—well, just how many of the fellows do such things of their own accord, for the fun of it, without the others knowing anything? I dare say it's not so bad then."

"But you did it on being ordered to. You debased yourself. Just as if you had crawled into the muck because someone else wanted you to."

"Oh, I grant that. But I had to."

"No, you didn't have to."

"They would have beaten me and reported me. Think how I would have got into disgrace."

"All right then, let's leave that. There's something else I want to know. Listen. I know you've spent a lot of money with Božena. You've boasted to her and thrown your weight about and made out what a man you are. So you want to be a man? Not just boasting and pretending to be—but with your whole soul? Now look, then suddenly someone demands such a humiliating service from you, and in the same moment you feel you're too cowardly to say no—doesn't it make a split go through

155

your whole being? A horror—something you can't describe—as though something unutterable had happened inside you?"

"Lord! I don't know what you mean. I don't know what you're getting at. I can't tell you anything —anything at all—about that."

"Now attend. I'm going to order you to get undressed again."

Basini smiled.

"And to lie down flat on the floor there in front of me. Don't laugh! I'm really ordering you to! D'you *hear* me? If you don't obey instantly, you'll see what you're in for when Reiting comes back! . . . That's right. So now you're lying naked on the ground in front of me. You're trembling, too. Are you cold? I could spit on your naked body now if I wanted to. Just press your head right on to the floor. Doesn't the dust on the boards look queer? Like a landscape full of clouds and lumps of rock as big as houses? I could stick pins into you. There are still some over there in the corner, by the lamp. D'you feel them in your skin even now? . . . But I don't mean to do that. I could make you bark, the way Beineberg does, and make you eat dust like a pig, I could make you do movements—oh, you know—and at the same time you would have to sigh : "Oh, my dear Moth——!" But Törless broke off abruptly in the midst of this sacrilege. "But I don't mean to—don't mean to—do you understand?"

Basini wept. "You're tormenting me . . ."

"Yes, I'm tormenting you. But that's not what I'm after. There's just one thing I want to know : when I drive all that into you like knives, what goes on in you? What happens inside you? Does something burst in you? Tell me! Does it smash like a glass that suddenly flies into thousands of splinters before there's been even a little crack in it ?   Doesn't the picture you've made of yourself go out like a candle ?   Doesn't something else leap into its place, the way the pictures in the magic-lantern leap out of the darkness ?   Don't you *understand* what I mean ?   I can't explain it for you any better. You must tell me yourself. . . ! "

Basini wept without stopping.   His girlish shoulders jerked.   All he could get out was to the same effect : " I don't know what you're after, I can't explain anything to you, it happens just in a moment, and then nothing different can happen, you'd do just the same as me."

Törless was silent.   He remained leaning against the wall, exhausted, motionless, blankly staring straight in front of him.

'If you were in my situation, you would do just the same,' Basini had said.   Seen thus, what had happened appeared a simple necessity, straightforward and un-complicated.

Törless's self-awareness rebelled in blazing contempt against the mere suggestion.   And yet this rebellion on the part of his whole being seemed to offer him no satisfactory guarantee . . .   ' . . . yes, *I* should have more character than he has, *I* shouldn't put up with such outrageous demands—but does it really matter ?   Does it matter that I should act differently, from firmness, from decency, from—oh, for all sorts of reasons that at the moment don't interest me in the least ?   No, what counts is not how I should act, but the fact that if I were ever really to act as Basini has done, I should have just as little sense of anything extraordinary about it as he has.   This is the heart of the matter : my feeling about myself would be exactly as simple and clear of ambiguity as his feeling about himself . . .'

This thought—flashing through his mind in half-coherent snatches of sentences that ran over into each other and kept beginning all over again—added to his contempt for Basini a very private, quiet pain that touched his inmost balance at a much deeper point than any moral consideration could. It came from his awareness of a sensation he had briefly had before and which he could not get rid of. The fact was that when Basini's words revealed to him the danger potentially menacing him from Reiting and Beineberg, he had simply been startled. He had been startled as by a sudden assault, and without stopping to think had in a flash looked round for cover and a way of parrying the attack. That had been in the moment of a real danger; and the sensation it had caused him—those swift, unthinking impulses —exasperated and stimulated him. He tried, all in vain, to set them off again. But he knew they had immediately deprived the danger of all its peculiarity and ambiguity.

And yet it had been the same danger that he had had a foreboding of only some weeks previously, in this same place—that time when he had felt so oddly startled by the lair itself, which was like some forgotten scrap of the Middle Ages lying remote from the warm, bright-lit life of the class-rooms, and by Beineberg and Reiting, because they seemed to have changed from the people they were down there, suddenly turning into something else, something sinister, blood-thirsty, figures in some quite different sort of life. That had been a transformation, a leap, for Törless, as though the picture of his surroundings had suddenly loomed up before other eyes—eyes just awakened out of a hundred years of sleep.

And yet it had been the same danger. . . . He kept on repeating this to himself. And ever and again he tried to compare the memories of the two different sensations. . . .

Meanwhile Basini had got up. Observing his companion's blank, absent gaze, he quietly took his clothes and slipped away.

Törless saw it happening—as though through a mist —but he uttered no word and let it go at that.

His attention was wholly concentrated on this straining to rediscover the point in himself where the change of inner perspective had suddenly occurred.

But every time he came anywhere near it the same thing happened to him as happens to someone trying to compare the close-at-hand with the remote : he could never seize the memory images of the two feelings together. For each time something came in between. It was like a faint click in the mind, corresponding more or less to something that occurs in the physical realm—that scarcely perceptible muscular sensation which is associated with the focusing of the gaze. And each time, precisely in the decisive moment, this would claim all his attention : the activity of making the comparison thrust itself before the objects to be compared, there was an almost unnoticeable jerk—and everything stopped.

So Törless kept on beginning all over again.

This mechanically regular operation lulled him into a rigid, waking, ice-cold sleep, holding him transfixed where he was—and for an indefinite period.

Then an idea wakened him like the light touch of a warm hand. It was an idea apparently so obvious and natural that he marvelled at its not having occurred to him long ago.

It was an idea that did nothing at all beyond generalising the experience he had just had : what in the distance seems so great and mysterious comes up to us always as something plain and undistorted, in natural, everyday proportions. It is as if there were an invisible frontier round every man . . . What originates outside and approaches from a long way off is like a misty sea full of gigantic, ever-changing forms ; what comes right up to any man, and becomes action, and collides with his life, is clear and small, human in its dimensions and human in its outlines. And between the life one lives and the life one feels, the life one only has inklings and glimpses of, seeing it only from afar, there lies that invisible frontier, and in it the narrow gateway where all that ever happens, the images of things, must throng together and shrink so that they can enter into a man . . .

And yet, closely though this corresponded to his experience, Törless let his head sink, deep in thought.

It seemed a queer idea . . .

AT last he was back in bed. He was not thinking of anything at all any more, for thinking came so hard and was so futile. What he had discovered about the secret contrivings of his friends did, it was true, go through his mind, but now as indifferently and lifelessly as an item of foreign news read in a newspaper.

There was nothing more to be hoped from Basini. Oh, there was still his problem! But that was so dubious, and he was so tired and mangled. An illusion perhaps—the whole thing.

Only the vision of Basini, of his bare, glimmering skin, left a fragrance, as of lilac, in that twilight of the sensations which comes just before sleep. Even the moral revulsion faded away. And at last Törless fell asleep.

*   *   *

No dream disturbed him. There was only an infinitely pleasant warmth spreading soft carpets under his body. After a while he woke out of it. And then he almost screamed. There, sitting on his bed, was Basini! And in the next instant, with crazy speed, Basini had flung off his night-clothes and slid under the blankets and was pressing his naked, trembling body against Törless.

As soon as Törless recovered from the shock, he pushed Basini away from him.

"What do you think you're doing——?"

But Basini pleaded. "Oh, don't start being like that

again ! Nobody's the way you are ! They don't despise me the way you do. They only pretend they do, so as to be different then afterwards. But you—you of all people ! You're even younger than me, even if you are stronger. We're both younger than the others. You don't boast and bully the way they do . . . You're gentle . . . I love you . . ."

"Here, I say ! I don't know what you're talking about ! I don't know what you want ! Go away ! Oh, go *away* ! " And in anguish Törless pushed his arm against Basini's shoulder, holding him off. But the hot proximity of the soft skin, this other person's skin, haunted him, enclosing him, suffocating him. And Basini kept on whispering : " Oh yes . . . oh yes . . . please . . . oh, I should so gladly do whatever you want ! "

* * *

Törless could find nothing to say to this. While Basini went on whispering and he himself was lost in doubt and consideration, something had sunk over his senses again like a deep green sea. Only Basini's flickering words shone out in it like the glint of little silvery fishes.

He was still holding Basini off with his arms. But something made them heavy, like a moist, torpid warmth; the muscles in them were slackening . . . he forgot them. . . . Only when another of those darting words touched him did he start awake again, all at once feeling —like something fearful and incomprehensible—that this very instant, as in a dream, his hands had drawn Basini closer.

Then he wanted to shake himself into wakefulness, wanted to shout at himself : Basini's tricking you, he's just trying to drag you down to where he is, so that you can't despise him any more! But the cry was never uttered, nor was there any sound anywhere in the whole huge building; throughout the corridors the dark tides of silence seemed to lie motionless in sleep.

He struggled to get back to himself. But those tides were like black sentinels at all the doors.

Then Törless abandoned his search for words. Lust, which had been slowly seeping into him, emanating from every single moment of desperation, had now grown to its full stature. It lay naked at his side and covered his head with its soft black cloak. And into his ear it whispered sweet words of resignation, while its warm fingers thrust all questionings and obligations aside as futile. And it whispered : In solitude you can do what you will.

Only in the moment when he was swept away he woke fleetingly, frantically clutching at the one thought : This is not myself! It's not me ! . . . But tomorrow it will be me again ! . . . Tomorrow . . .

ON Tuesday evening the first of the other boys returned. The rest were arriving only by the night trains. There was unceasing bustle in the building.

Törless met his friends curtly and sullenly ; he had not forgotten. And then, too, they came back bringing from outside such a whiff of vigour and man-of-the-world confidence. It shamed him, who now cared only for the stuffy air between four narrow walls.

He was, indeed, often ashamed now. But it was not actually so much because of what he had let himself be seduced into doing—for that was nothing so very rare at boarding-school—as because he now found he could not quite help having a kind of tenderness for Basini, while on the other hand he felt more intensely than ever how despised and humiliated this creature was.

He quite often had secret meetings with him. He took him to all the hiding-places he had learnt of from Beineberg, and since he himself was not good at such furtive adventurings, Basini soon knew the way everywhere better than he did and became the leader.

But at night he could not rest for jealousy, keeping watch on Beineberg and Reiting.

These two, however, held aloof from Basini. Perhaps they were already bored with him. At any rate, some change seemed to have taken place in them. Beineberg had become gloomy and reserved ; when he spoke, it was only to throw out mysterious hints of something that was imminent. Reiting seemed to have diverted his interest to other things; with his usual deftness he was again weaving the web for some plot or other, trying to win over some by doing them little favours and frightening others by showing them that— by some obscure cunning of his own—he knew their secrets.

However, when the three of them were at last alone together, the other two urged that Basini should very soon be given orders to appear once more in the cubby-hole or the attic.

Törless tried, on all sorts of pretexts, to postpone this, and at the same time suffered ceaselessly because of this secret sympathy for Basini.

Even a few weeks earlier such a state of mind would have been utterly alien to him; for he came of sturdy, sound, and natural stock.

But it would be entirely wrong to believe that Basini had aroused in Törless a desire that was—however fleetingly and perplexedly—a thorough-going and real one. True, something like passion had been aroused in him, but 'love' was quite certainly only a casual, haphazard term for it, and the boy Basini himself was no more than a substitute, a provisional object of this longing. For although Törless did debase himself with him, his desire was never satisfied by him; on the contrary, it went on growing out beyond Basini, growing out into some new and aimless craving.

*   *   *

At first it had been purely and simply the nakedness of the boy's slim body that dazzled him.

The feeling it had given him was no different from what he would have felt had he been confronted with the naked body of a little girl, a body still utterly sexless,

165

merely beautiful. It had been an overwhelming shock
. . . a state of marvel . . . And the inevitable purity
of this feeling was what lent the appearance of affection—
this new and wonderfully uneasy emotion—to his relationship with Basini. Everything else had little to do
with it. All the other feelings—the erotic desire itself—
had been there long before ; it had all been there much
earlier, indeed even before he had come to know Božena.
It was the secret, aimless, melancholy sensuality of
adolescence, a sensuality attaching itself to no person,
and like the moist, black, sprouting earth in early spring,
or like dark, subterranean waters that some chance event
will cause to rise, sweeping the walls away.

The experience that Törless had gone through turned
out to be this event. Surprise, misunderstanding, confusion about his own feelings, all combined to smash
open the hushed hiding-places where all that was secret,
taboo, torrid, vague and solitary in his soul was accumu-
lated, and to send the flood of dark stirrings moving out in
Basini's direction. And here it was that for the first
time they encountered something warm, something that
breathed and was fragrant, was flesh, in which these
vaguely roving dreams took on form and had their
share in the beauty of the flesh, instead of in squalor such
as they had been blighted with, in the depths of his
loneliness, by his experience with Božena. This now all
at once flung open a gate, a way ahead into life, and in the
half-light of this condition everything now mingled—
wishes and reality, debauched fantasies and instant
impressions that still bore the warm traces of life itself,
stimuli from without, and flames that came flaring up
from within, mantling the sensations in such a glare that
they were unrecognisable.

But all this was beyond Törless's own power of dis-
crimination ; for him it was all run together in a single,

blurred, undifferentiated emotion, which in his first surprise he might well take for love.

*   *   *

It was not long before he learnt to evaluate it more
accurately.   From then on he was restlessly driven hither
and thither by uneasiness.   Every object he picked up
he laid down again as soon as he had touched it.   He
could not talk to any of the other boys without falling
inexplicably silent or absent-mindedly changing the subject several times.   It would also happen sometimes
that while he was speaking a wave of shame flooded
through him, so that he grew red, began to stammer,
and had to turn away. . . .

By day he avoided Basini.   When he could not help
looking at him, it almost always had a sobering effect.
Every movement of Basini's filled him with disgust, the
vague shadows of his illusions gave way to a cold, blunt
lucidity, and his soul seemed to shrivel up until there
was nothing left but the memory of a former desire that
now seemed unspeakably senseless and repulsive.   He
would stamp his foot and double up as if thus he could
escape from this anguish of shame.

He wondered what the others would say to him if
they knew his secret—what would his parents say?—
and the masters?

But this last turn of the knife always put an end to his
torments.   A cool weariness would then come over
him; the hot, slack skin of his body would then grow
taut again in a pleasurable cold shiver.   At such times
he would be still and let everyone pass him by.   But
there was in him a certain contempt for them all.
Secretly he suspected the very worst of everyone he
spoke to.

And he imagined, into the bargain, that he could see

no trace of shame in them. He did not think that they suffered as he knew he did. The crown of thorns that his tormented conscience set on his own brow seemed to be missing from theirs.

Yet he felt like one who had awakened from the throes of some long agony—like one who had been brushed by the silent and mysterious finger-tips of dissolution—like one who cannot forget the tranquil wisdom of a long illness.

This was a state in which he felt happy, and the moments came again and again when he yearned for it.

They always began with his once more being able to look at Basini with indifference and to face out the loathsome and beastly thing with a smile. Then he knew that he *would* debase himself, but he supplied it all with a new meaning. The uglier and unworthier everything was that Basini had to offer him, the greater was the contrast with that awareness of suffering sensibility which would afterwards set in.

Törless would withdraw into some corner from which he could observe without himself being seen. When he shut his eyes, a vague sense of urgency would rise up in him, and when he opened his eyes he could find nothing that corresponded to it. And then suddenly the thought of Basini would loom up and concentrate everything in itself. Soon it would lose all definite outline. It seemed no longer to belong to him, and seemed no longer to refer to Basini. It was something that was encircled by a whirling throng of emotions, as though by lecherous women in high-necked long robes, with masks over their faces.

Törless knew no name for any of these emotions, nor did he know what any of them portended; but it was precisely in this that the intoxicating fascination lay. He no longer knew himself; and out of this very fact his urge grew into a wild, contemptuous debauchery, as when at some *fête galante* the lights are suddenly put out and nobody knows who it is he pulls down to the ground and covers with kisses.

*   *   *

Later, when he had got over his adolescent experiences, Törless became a young man whose mind was both subtle and sensitive. By that time he was one of those æsthetically inclined intellectuals who find there is something soothing in a regard for law and indeed—to some extent at least—for public morals too, since it frees them from the necessity of ever thinking about anything coarse, anything that is remote from the finer spiritual processes. And yet the magnificent external correctitude of these people, with its slight touch of irony, at once becomes associated with boredom and callousness if they are expected to show any more personal interest in particular instances of the workings of law and morality. For the only real interest they feel is concentrated on the growth of their own soul, or personality, or whatever one may call the thing within us that every now and then increases by the addition of some idea picked up between the lines of a book, or which speaks to us in the silent language of a painting the thing that every now and then awakens when some solitary, wayward tune floats past us and away, away into the distance, whence with alien movements tugs at the thin scarlet thread of our blood—the thing that is never there when we are writing minutes, building machines, going to the circus, or following any of the hundreds of other similar occupations.

And so to such people the things that make demands only on their moral correctitude are of the utmost indifference. This was why in his later life Törless never felt remorse for what had happened at that time. His tastes had become so acutely and one-sidedly focused on matters purely of the mind that, supposing he had been told a very similar story about some rake's debaucheries, it would certainly never have occurred to him to direct his indignation against the acts themselves. He would have despised such a person not for being a debauchee, but for being nothing more than that; not for his licentiousness, but for the psychological condition that made him do those things; for being stupid, or because his intellect lacked any emotional counter-weight— that is to say, despising him always only for the picture he presented of something miserable, deprived, and feeble. And he would have despised him in exactly the same way whether his vice lay in sexual debauchery, or in uncontrolled and excessive cigarette-smoking, or in drinking.

And as is the case with all people who are exclusively concerned with heightening their mental faculties, the mere presence of voluptuous and unbridled urges did not count for much with him. It was a pet notion of his that the capacity for enjoyment, and creative talent, and in fact the whole more highly developed side of the inner life, was a piece of jewellery on which one could easily injure oneself. He regarded it as inevitable that a person with a rich and varied inner life experienced moments of which other people must know nothing, and memories that he kept in secret drawers. And all he himself expected of such a person was the ability to make exquisite use of them afterwards.

And so, when somebody whom he once told the story of his youth asked him whether the memory of that episode did not sometimes make him feel uncomfortable, he answered, with a smile: "Of course I don't deny that it was a degrading affair. And why not? The degradation passed off. And yet it left something behind

—that small admixture of a toxic substance which is needed to rid the soul of its over-confident, complacent healthiness, and to give it instead a sort of health that is more acute, and subtler, and wiser.

" And anyway, would you try to count the hours of degradation that leave their brand-marks on the soul after every great passion ? You need only think of the hours of deliberate humiliation in love—those rapt hours when lovers bend down as though leaning over a deep well, or one lays his ear on the other's heart, listening for the sound of impatient claws as the restless great cats scratch on their prison walls. And only in order to feel their own trembling ! Only in order to feel terrified at their loneliness up there above those dark, corroding depths ! Only—in their dread of being alone with those sinister forces—to take refuge wholly in each other !

" Just look young married couples straight in the eyes. What those eyes say is : So that's what you think, is it ?—oh, but you've no notion how deep we can sink ! What those eyes express is light-hearted mockery of anyone who knows nothing of so much that they know, and the affectionate pride of those who have gone together through all the circles of hell.

" And just as such lovers go that way together, so I at that time went through all those things, but on my own."

* * *

Nevertheless, even if that was Törless's view of it later on, at this time, when he was still exposed to the storm of solitary, yearning feelings, he was far from always being confident that everything would turn out all right in the end. The enigmas that had been tormenting him only a short time ago were still having a vague after-effect, which went on vibrating in the background of his experiences, like a deep note resounding

171

from afar. These were the very things he did not want to think of now.

But at times he remembered it all. And then he would be overwhelmed with utter despair, and was at the mercy of a quite different, weary, hopeless sense of shame.

Yet he could not account for this either.

The reason for it lay in the particular conditions of life at this school. Here youthful, upsurging energies were held captive behind grey walls and, having no other outlet, they filled the imagination with random wanton fancies that caused more than one boy to lose his head.

A certain degree of debauchery was even considered manly, dashing, a bold gesture of taking for oneself the pleasures one was still forbidden. And it seemed all the manlier when compared with the wretchedly respectable appearance of most of the masters. For then the admonishing word ' morality ' became ludicrously associated with narrow shoulders, a little paunch, thin legs, and eyes roaming as harmlessly behind their spectacles as the silly sheep at pasture, as though life were nothing but a flowery meadow of solemn edification.

And, finally, at school one still had no knowledge of life and no notion of all those degrees of beastliness and corruption, down to the level of the diseased and the grotesque, which are what primarily fills the adult with revulsion when he hears of such things.

All these inhibiting factors, which are far more effective than we can really appreciate, were lacking in him. It was his very naivety that had plunged him into vice.

For the moral force of resistance, that sensitive faculty of the spirit which he was later to rate so high, was not yet developed in him either. However, there were already signs of its growth. True, Törless went astray, seeing as yet only the shadows cast ahead into his consciousness by something still unrecognised, and mistaking them for reality : but he had a task to fulfil where he himself was concerned, a spiritual task—even if he was still not equipped to undertake it.

All he knew was that he had been following something as yet undefined along a road that led deep into his inner being ; and in doing so he had grown tired. He had got into the way of hoping for extraordinary, mysterious discoveries, and that habit had brought him into the narrow, winding passages of sensuality. It was all the result not of perversity, but of a psychological situation in which he had lost his sense of direction.

And this disloyalty to something in himself that was serious and worth striving for was the very thing that filled him with a vague sense of guilt. An indefinable hidden disgust never quite left him, and an indistinct dread pursued him like one who in the dark no longer knows whether he is still walking along his chosen road or has lost it, not knowing where.

Then he would endeavour not to think of anything at all. He drifted through life, dumb and bemused and oblivious of all his earlier questionings. The subtle enjoyment that lay in his acts of degradation became ever rarer.

It had not yet left him entirely ; but still, at the end of this period Törless did not even try to oppose when further decisions were taken regarding Basini's fate.

THIS happened some days later, when the three of them were together in the cubby-hole. Beineberg was very grave.

Reiting spoke first: "Beineberg and I think things can't go on as they have been going in the matter of Basini. He's got used to being at our beck and call. It doesn't make him miserable any more. He's become as impudently familiar as a servant. So it's time to go a step further with him. Do you agree?"

"Well, I don't even know yet what you mean to do with him."

"Yes, it isn't so easy to work that out. We must humiliate him still more and make him knuckle under completely. I should like to see how far it can go. The question is only how to do it. Of course I have one or two rather nice ideas about it. For instance, we could give him a flogging and make him sing psalms of thanksgiving at the same time—it would be a song well worth hearing, I think—every note covered with gooseflesh, so to speak. We could make him bring us the filthiest things in his mouth, like a dog. Or we could take him along to Božena's and make him read his mother's letters aloud while Božena provided the suitable kind of jokes to go with it. But there's plenty of time to think about all that. We can turn it over in our minds, polish it up, and keep on adding new refinements. Without the appropriate details it's still a bit of a bore, for the present. Perhaps we'll hand him right over to the class to deal with. That would be the most sensible thing to do. If each one of so many contributes even a little, it'll be enough to tear him to pieces. And anyway, I have a liking for these mass movements. Nobody means to contribute anything spectacular, and yet the waves keep rising higher and higher, until they break over everyone's head. You chaps just wait and see, nobody will lift a finger, but all the same there'll be a terrific upheaval. Instigating a thing like that gives me really quite particular pleasure."

"But what do you mean to do first of all?"

"As I said, I should like to save *that* up for later. For the time being I should be content with softening him up again in every respect, either by threats or by beating him."

"What for?" Törless asked before he could stop himself.

They looked each other straight in the eye.

"Oh, don't go and play the innocent!" Reiting said. "You know perfectly well what I'm talking about."

Törless said nothing. How much had Reiting found out? Or was he only taking a shot in the dark?

"Don't tell me you've forgotten what Beineberg told you that time—about what Basini will lend himself to."

Törless drew a breath of relief.

"Well, there's nothing to look so amazed about. You gaped just the same that time, too, but it's not as if it were anything so very frightful. Incidentally, Beineberg does the same with Basini—he's told me so himself." And Reiting looked across at Beineberg with an ironical grimace. That was very much his way: he had no scruple about giving somebody else away in public.

Beineberg did not respond at all. He remained sitting in his thoughtful attitude, scarcely glancing up.

" Well, aren't you going to come out with your idea ? " Reiting said to Beineberg, and then, turning to Törless, he went on : " The fact is he has a crazy notion he wants to try out on Basini, and he's set on doing it before we do anything else. I must say it's quite an amusing one, too."

Beineberg remained grave. He now looked hard at Törless and said : " You remember what we talked about that time behind the coats ? "

" Yes."

" I never got talking about it again, because after all there's no point in just talking. But I've often thought about it—I assure you, often. And what Reiting has just been telling you is true too. I've done the same with Basini as he has. In fact, perhaps a bit more. And that was because, as I told you that time, I believe sex may perhaps be the right gateway. It was a sort of experiment. I didn't see any other way to get to what I was looking for. But there's no sense in this random sort of going on. I've been thinking about it—for nights on end—trying to work out how one could put something systematic in the place of it.

" Now I think I've got it, and we shall make the experiment. Now you will see too how wrong you were that time. All our knowledge of the universe is doubtful. Everything really works differently. At that time we discovered this, so to speak, from the reverse side, in looking for points where the perfectly natural explanation falls over its own feet. But now I trust I am able to demonstrate the positive side—the other side ! "

Reiting set out the tea-cups. As he did so, he nudged Törless cheerfully. " Now pay attention. It's a pretty smart thing he's thought up ! "

But Beineberg made a quick movement and extinguished the lamp. In the darkness there was only the flame of the spirit-stove, casting flickering bluish gleams on their faces.

"I put the lamp out, Törless, because it is better to talk about such things in the dark. And you, Reiting, can go to sleep for all I care, if you're too stupid to understand profounder things."

Reiting laughed as if he were amused.

"Well," Beineberg began, "you remember our conversation. At that time you yourself had discovered that little peculiarity in mathematics, that example of the fact that our thinking has no even, solid, safe basis, but goes along, as it were, over holes in the ground—shutting its eyes, ceasing to exist for a moment, and yet arriving safely at the other side. Really we ought to have despaired long ago, for in all fields our knowledge is streaked with such crevasses—nothing but fragments drifting in a fathomless ocean.

"But we do not despair. We go on feeling as safe as if we were on firm ground. If we didn't have this solid feeling of certainty, we would kill ourselves in desperation about the wretchedness of our intellect. This feeling is with us continually, holding us together, and at every moment protectively taking our intellect into its arms like a small child. As soon as we have become aware of this, we cannot go on denying the existence of the soul. As soon as we analyse our mental life and recognise the inadequacy of the intellect, we feel all this very clearly. We feel it—do you understand? For if it were not for this feeling, we should collapse like empty sacks.

"Only we have forgotten to pay attention to this feeling. But it is one of the oldest feelings there is. Even thousands of years ago peoples living thousands of miles apart from each other knew of it. Once one has begun to take an interest in these things, one can no longer deny them. But I don't want to talk you into believing what I believe. I'm only going to tell you the bare essentials, so that you won't be quite unprepared. The facts themselves will provide the proof.

" Now, assuming that the soul exists, it follows as a matter of course—doesn't it ?—that we cannot have any deeper longing than to restore the lost contact with it, become familiar with it again, learn to make better use of its powers again, and gain for ourselves a share in the supernatural forces that are dormant in its depths.

" For all this is possible. It has been done more than once. The miracles, the saints, and the holy men of India—they all bear witness to such events."

" Look here," Törless interjected, " you're rather talking yourself into believing this, aren't you ? You had to put the lamp out specially so that you could. But would you talk just the same if we were sitting downstairs among the others, who are doing their geography or history or writing letters home, where the light is bright and the usher may come round between the desks ? Wouldn't this talk of yours seem a bit fantastic even to yourself there, a bit presumptuous, as though we were not the same as the others, but were living in another world, say eight hundred years ago ? "

" No, my dear Törless, I should maintain the same things. Incidentally, it's one of your faults that you're always looking at what the others are doing. You're not independent enough. Writing letters home ! Thinking of your parents where such things are concerned ! What reason have you to believe they could at all follow us here ? We are young, we are a generation later, and perhaps things are destined for us that they never dreamt of in all their lives. At least, I feel that it is so.

" Still, what's the use of going on talking ? I shall prove it to you both anyway."

After they had been silent for a while, Törless said :
" And how, if it comes to that, do you mean to set about
getting hold of your soul ? "

" I'm not going to explain that to you now, all the
more since I shall have to do it in front of Basini anyway."

" But you could at least give us some sort of idea."

" Well, it's like this. History teaches that there is
only one way : entering into one's own being in meditation. Only this is where the difficulty begins. The
saints of old, for instance, at the time when the soul still
manifested itself in miracles, were able to reach this goal
by means of fervent prayer. The fact is at that time the
soul was of a different nature. Now that way is not
open to us. Today we don't know what to do. The
soul has changed, and unfortunately between then and
now there lie times when nobody paid proper attention
to the subject and the tradition was irrevocably lost. We
can only find a new way by means of most careful thought.
This is what I have been intensively occupied with
recently. The most obvious choice is probably to do it
by the aid of hypnosis. Only it has never yet been tried.
All they do is keep on performing the same commonplace tricks, which is why the methods haven't yet been
tested for their capacity to lead towards higher things.
The final thing I want to say now is that I shall not
hypnotise Basini by the usual methods but according to
one of my own, which, if I am not mistaken, is similar
to one that was used in the Middle Ages."

" Isn't Beineberg a treat ? " Reiting exclaimed, laughing. " Only he ought to have lived in the age when
they went round prophesying the end of the world.
Then he would have ended up by really believing it was
due to his soul-magic that the world remained intact."

When Törless looked at Beineberg after these mocking
words, he saw that his face was quite rigid and distorted

as though convulsed with concentration, and in the next moment he felt the touch of ice-cold fingers. He was startled by this high degree of excitement. But then the tension relaxed, the grip on his arm slackened.

"Oh, it was nothing," Beineberg said. "Just an idea. I felt as though something special were just going to occur to me, a clue to how to do it. . . ."

"I say, you really are a bit touched," Reiting said jovially. "You always used to be a tough sort of chap, you only went in for all this stuff as a sort of game. But now you're like an old woman."

"Oh, leave me alone—you've no idea what it means to know such things are at hand and to be on the point of reaching them today or any day now!"

"Stop quarrelling," Törless said. In the course of the last few weeks he had become a good deal firmer and more energetic. "For all I care each of you can do what he likes. I don't believe in anything at all—neither in your crafty tortures, Reiting, nor in Beineberg's hopes. For my own part, I have nothing to say. I'm simply going to wait and see what you two produce."

"So when shall it be?"

The night after the next was decided on.

TÖRLESS made no resistance to its approach. And indeed in this new situation his feeling for Basini had completely died out. This was quite fortunate for him, since at least it freed him all at once from the wavering between shame and desire that he had been unable to get out of by exerting his own strength. Now at least he had a straightforward, plain repugnance for Basini; it was as if the humiliations intended for the latter might be capable of defiling him too.

For the rest he was absent-minded and could not bring himself to think of anything seriously, least of all about the things that had once so intensely preoccupied him.

Only when he went upstairs to the attic together with Reiting—Beineberg and Basini having gone ahead—the memory of what had once gone on in him became more vivid again. He could not rid himself of the sound of the cocksure words he had flung at Beineberg, and he yearned to regain that confidence. He lingered a little on each of the stairs, dragging his feet. But his former certainty would not return. Though he recalled all the thoughts he had had at that time, they seemed to pass him by, remote as though they were no more than the shadowy images of what he had once thought.

Finally, since he found nothing in himself, his curiosity turned again to the events that were to come from outside; and this impelled him forward.

Swiftly he followed Reiting, hurrying up the last of the stairs.

While the iron door was groaning shut behind them, he felt, with a sigh, that though Beineberg's plan might be only laughable hocus-pocus, at least there was something firm and deliberate about it, whereas everything in himself lay in impenetrable confusion and perplexity.

Tense with expectation, they sat down on one of the horizontal beams, as though in a theatre.

Beineberg was already there with Basini.

The situation seemed favourable to his plan. The darkness, the stale air, the foul, brackish smell emanating from the water-tubs, all this generated a feeling of drowsiness, of never being able to wake up again, a weary, sluggish indolence.

Beineberg told Basini to undress. Now in the darkness Basini's naked skin had a bluish, mouldy glimmer; there was nothing in the least provocative about it.

Suddenly Beineberg pulled the revolver out of his pocket and aimed it at Basini.

Even Reiting leaned forward as though preparing to leap between the two of them at any moment.

But Beineberg was smiling—smiling in a strangely distorted way, as though he did not really mean to at all, but rather as if fanatical words welling up in him had twisted his lips into a queer grimace.

Basini had dropped to his knees, as though paralysed, and was staring at the gun, his eyes wide with fear.

"Get up," Beineberg said. "If you do exactly what I tell you, you won't come to any harm. But if you disturb me by making the slightest difficulty, I shall shoot you down like a dog. Take note of that!

"As a matter of fact, I am going to kill you anyway, but you'll come back to life again. Dying is not so alien to us as you think it is. We die every day—in our deep, dreamless sleep."

Once again the wild smile distorted Beineberg's mouth.

"Now kneel down, up there "—he pointed to a wide horizontal beam that ran across the attic at about waist-level—" that's it—quite straight—hold yourself perfectly straight—keep your shoulders back. And now keep looking at this—but no blinking! You must keep your eyes open as wide as you possibly can!"

Beineberg put a little spirit-lamp in front of Basini in such a position that he had to bend his head back slightly in order to look right into the flame.

It was difficult to make anything out exactly in the dimness, but after some time it seemed that Basini's body was beginning to swing to and fro like a pendulum. The bluish gleams were flickering on his skin. Now and then Törless thought he could see Basini's face, contorted with terror.

After a time Beineberg asked: "Are you feeling tired?"

The question was put in the usual way that hypnotists put it.

Then he began explaining, his voice low and husky:

"Dying is only a result of our way of living. We live from one thought to the next, from one feeling to the next. Our thoughts and feelings don't flow along quietly like a stream, they 'occur' to us, which means they 'run against' us, crash into us like stones that have been thrown. If you watch yourself carefully, you'll realise that the soul isn't something that changes its colours in smooth gradations, but that the thoughts jump out of it like numbers out of a black hole. Now you have a thought or a feeling, and all at once there's a different one there, as if it had popped up out of nothingness. If you pay attention, you can even notice the instant between two thoughts when everything's black. For us that instant—once we have grasped it—is simply death.

183

"For our life is nothing but setting milestones and hopping from one to the next, hopping over thousands of death-seconds every day. We live as it were only in the points of rest. And that is why we have such a ridiculous dread of irrevocable death, for that is the thing that is absolutely without milestones, the fathomless abyss that we fall into. It is in fact the utter negation of this kind of living.

"But it is so only if it is looked at from the point of view of this kind of living, and only for the person who has not learnt to experience himself otherwise than from moment to moment.

"I call this The Hopping Evil, and the secret lies in overcoming it. One must awaken the feeling of one's own life in oneself as of something peacefully gliding along. In the moment when this really happens one is just as near to death as to life. One ceases to live—in our earthly sense of the word—but one cannot die any more either, for with the cancelling out of life one has also cancelled out death. This is the instant of immortality, the instant when the soul steps out of our narrow brain into the wonderful gardens of its own life.

"So now pay close attention to what I say.

"Put all your thoughts to sleep, keep staring into this little flame . . . Don't think from one thing to another . . . Concentrate all your attention in an inward direction . . . Keep staring at the flame . . . Your thoughts are slowing down, like an engine gradually running slower and slower . . . slower . . . and . . . slower . . . Keep staring inward . . . Keep on staring . . . till you find the point where you feel yourself, feeling without any thought or sensation . . .

"Your silence will be all the answer I want. Don't avert your gaze from within!"

Minutes passed.

"Do you feel the point . . .?"

No answer.

"Do you hear, Basini, have you done it?"

Silence.

Beineberg stood up, and his gaunt shadow rose high beside the beam. Up above, Basini's body could be seen rocking to and fro, drunk with darkness.

"Turn sideways," Beineberg ordered. "What obeys now is only the brain," he murmured, "the brain, which still goes on functioning mechanically for a while, until the last traces of what the soul imprinted on it are consumed. The soul itself is somewhere else—in its next form of existence. It is no longer wearing the fetters of the laws of Nature." He turned to Törless for a moment : "It is no longer condemned to the punishment of making a body heavy and holding it together. Bend forward, Basini—that's right—slowly, slowly. And a bit further. A bit further still. As the last trace is extinguished in the brain, the muscles will relax and the empty body will collapse. Or it will simply float, I don't know which. The soul has left the body of its own accord. This is not the ordinary sort of death. Perhaps the body will float in the air because there's nothing left in possession of it—no force either of life or of death. Bend forward . . . And a bit more."

*   *   *

At this moment Basini, who had been obeying all these commands out of sheer terror, lost his balance and crashed to the floor at Beineberg's feet.

Basini yelled with pain. Reiting burst out laughing. But Beineberg, who had fallen back a step, uttered a gurgling cry of rage when he realised that he had been tricked. With a swift movement he ripped his leather belt from his waist, seized Basini by the hair, and began

185

lashing him furiously. All the tremendous tension he had been under now found release in these frantic blows. And Basini howled with pain, so that the attic rang with lamentation as if a dog were howling.

*   *   *

Törless had sat in silence during the whole of the previous scene. He had been secretly hoping that something might happen after all that would carry him back to the emotional realm he had lost. It was a foolish hope, as he had known all along, but it had held him spellbound. Now, however, it seemed to be all over. The scene revolted him. There was no longer any trace of thought in him, only mute, inert repugnance.

He got up quietly and left without saying a word, all quite mechanically.

Beineberg was still lashing away at Basini and would obviously go on doing so to the point of exhaustion.

WHEN Törless was in bed, he felt : This is the end of it. Something is over and done with.

During the next few days he went on quietly with his school work, not bothering about anything else. Reiting and Beineberg were probably now carrying out their programme item by item ; but he kept out of their way.

Then on the fourth day, when nobody happened to be there, Basini came up to him. He looked ghastly, his face was wan and thin, and in his eyes there was a feverish flicker of constant dread. Glancing nervously about him, he spoke hurriedly and in gasps : " You've got to help me ! You're the only person who can ! I can't stand any more of their tormenting me. I've stood everything up to now, but if it goes on like this they'll kill me ! "

Törless found it disagreeable to have to say anything in reply to this. At last he said : " I can't help you. It's all your own fault. You're to blame for what's happening to you."

" But only a short time ago you were still so nice and good to me."

" Never."

" But——"

" Shut up ! It wasn't me. It was a dream. A mood. It actually suits me quite well that your new disgrace has torn you away from me. For me it's better that way. . . ."

Basini let his head sink. He realised that a sea of grey

and sober disappointment lay now between him and Törless. . . . Törless was cold, a different person.

Then he threw himself down on his knees before Törless, beat his head on the floor and cried: " Help me! Help me! For God's sake help me!"

Törless hesitated for a moment. He felt neither any wish to help Basini nor enough indignation to push him away. So he acted on the first thought that occurred to him. " Come to the attic tonight. I'll talk it over with you again." But the next moment he was already regretting it.

' Why stir it all up again?' he wondered, and then said, as though on second thoughts: " But they'd notice. It can't be done."

" Oh no, they were up all last night with me, till dawn. They'll sleep tonight."

" All right then, for all I care. But don't expect me to help you."

* * *

It was against his own judgment that Törless had decided to meet Basini. For his real conviction was that inwardly it was all over—there was nothing more to be got out of it. Now only a sort of pedantry, some stubborn conscientiousness, had inspired him with the notion of again meddling with these things, even though he knew from the start that it was hopeless.

He felt the need to get it over quickly.

Basini did not know how he was expected to behave. He had been beaten so much that he scarcely dared to stir. Every trace of personality seemed to have gone out of him; only in his eyes there was still a little residue of it, and it peered out shakily, imploringly, as though clutching at Törless.

He waited to see what Törless would do.

Finally Törless broke the silence. He spoke rapidly, in a bored manner, as though it were merely for the sake of form that he was again going over a matter which had long been settled.

"I'm not going to help you. It's a fact, I did take an interest in you for a time, but that's over now. You're really nothing but a cowardly rotter. Definitely that's all you are. So what should make me take your part? I always used to think there must be some word, some feeling, I could find that would describe you differently. But there's really nothing that describes you better than saying you're a cowardly rotter. That's so simple and meaningless, and still it's all that can be said. Whatever else I wanted from you before, I've forgotten since you got in the way of it with your lecherous desires. I wanted to find a point remote from you, to look at you from there. That was my interest in you. You destroyed it yourself. But that's enough about that, I don't owe you any explanation. Only one more thing —what do you feel like now?"

"What do you expect me to feel like? I can't stand any more of it."

"I suppose they're doing pretty bad things to you now, and it hurts?"

"Yes."

"But just pain—is it as simple as that? You feel that you're suffering and you want to escape from it? Simply that, without any complications?"

Basini had no answer.

"Oh, all right, I was just asking by the way, not really formulating it precisely enough. Still, that doesn't matter. I have no more to do with you. I've already told you that. You don't arouse the slightest feeling in me any more. Do whatever you like."

Törless turned to go.

Then Basini tore his clothes off and thrust himself against Törless. His body was covered with weals. It was a disgusting sight, and his movements were as wretched as those of a clumsy prostitute. Nauseated, Törless shook him off and went.

But he had taken scarcely more than a few paces into the darkness when he collided with Reiting.

" What's all this ? So you have secret meetings with Basini, do you ? "

Törless followed Reiting's gaze, looking back at Basini. Just at the place where Basini was standing a broad beam of moonlight came in through a skylight, making the bluish-tinged skin with the weals on it look like the skin of a leper. As though he had to find some excuse for this sight, Törless said : " He asked me."

" What does he want ? "

" He wants me to protect him."

" Well, he's come to the right person, hasn't he ! "

" I might really do it, only the whole thing bores me."

Reiting glanced up, unpleasantly surprised. Then he turned angrily to Basini.

" We'll teach you to start secret plots against us ! And your guardian angel Törless will look on in person and enjoy it."

Törless had already turned away, but this piece of spite, so obviously aimed at him, held him back and, without stopping to think, he said :

" Look here, Reiting, I shall not do anything of the kind. I'm not going to have any more to do with it. I'm sick of the whole thing."

" All of a sudden ? "

" Yes, all of a sudden. Before, I was searching for something behind it all. . . ." He did not know why he said this or why now again it kept on coming back into his mind.

" Aha, second sight ! "

" Yes.   But now I can see only one thing—how vulgar and brutal you and Beineberg are."

" But you shall also see how Basini eats mud," Reiting sneered.

" That doesn't interest me any more."

" It certainly used to ! "

" I've already told you, only as long as Basini's state of mind was a riddle to me."

" And now ? "

" Now I don't know anything about riddles.   Things just happen : that's the sum total of wisdom."   Törless was surprised to find himself all at once again uttering phrases from that lost realm of feeling.   And so, when Reiting mockingly retorted that one did not have to travel far to pick up that sort of wisdom, an angry sense of superiority shot up in him and made him speak harshly.   For a moment he despised Reiting so much that he would really have enjoyed trampling him underfoot.

" Gibe away as much as you like.   But the things you two are up to are nothing more or less than brainless, senseless, disgusting torture of someone weaker than you are ! "

Reiting cast a sidelong glance at Basini, who was pricking up his ears.

" You mind what you say, Törless ! "

" Disgusting and filthy !   You heard what I said ! "

Now Reiting burst out too.   " I forbid you to be abusive about us in front of Basini ! "

" Oh, to hell with you !   Who are you to forbid anything ?   That time is over.   Once I used to respect you and Beineberg, but now I can see what you really are— stupid, revolting, beastly fools ! "

" Shut up, or——" and Reiting seemed about to leap at Törless.

Törless retreated slightly, yelling at him : " D'you think I'm going to fight with you ? You needn't think Basini's worth that to me ! Do what you like with him, but get out of my way ! "

Reiting seemed to have changed his mind about hitting Törless ; he stepped aside. He did not even touch Basini. But Törless knew him well enough to realise one thing : from now on all that was malicious and dangerous in Reiting would be a perpetual threat to him.

IT was in the afternoon, only two days later, that Reiting and Beineberg came up to Törless.

He saw the unpleasant look in their eyes. Obviously Beineberg now bore *him* a grudge for the ridiculous collapse of his prophecies, and Reiting had probably been egging him on, into the bargain.

" I hear you've been abusive about us. And in front of Basini, at that. Why ? "

Törless made no answer.

" You realise we are not going to put up with that sort of thing. But because it's you, and we're used to your odd whims, and don't attach overmuch importance to them, we're prepared to let it go at that. There's just one thing you have to do, though." In spite of the amiability of the words, there was something malevolently expectant in Beineberg's eyes.

" Basini's coming to the lair tonight. We're going to discipline him for having set you against us. When you see us leave the dormitory, come after us."

But Törless refused. " You two can do what you like. You'll have to leave me out of it."

" Tonight we're going to have our fun with Basini. for the last time, and tomorrow we're handing him over to the class, because he's beginning to be difficult."

" You can do whatever you like."

" But you're going to be there too."

" No."

" It's in front of you especially that Basini must see

nothing can help him against us. Only yesterday he was refusing to carry out our orders. We half thrashed him to death, but he stuck to it. We'll have to resort to moral means again, and humiliate him first in front of you and then in front of the class."

" But I'm not going to be there."

" Why not ? "

" I'm not going to be there, that's all."

Beineberg drew a deep breath ; it looked as if he were gathering together all the venom he had in him. Then he stepped up very close to Törless.

" Do you really think we don't know why ? Do you think we don't know how far you've gone with Basini ? "

" No further than you two."

" Indeed ? And I suppose that's why he chooses precisely you for his patron saint ? Eh ? That's why he has this great confidence precisely in you, is it ? You needn't think we're stupid enough to believe that ! "

Törless grew angry. " I don't care what you know, I don't want to have any more to do with your filthy goings-on ! "

" Oh, so you're getting impertinent again ! "

" You two make me sick ! Your beastliness is utterly senseless ! That's what's so revolting about you."

" Now listen to me. You ought to be grateful to us for quite a number of things. If you think that in spite of that you can now set yourself up above us, who have been your instructors, then you're making a grave mistake. Are you coming along tonight, yes or no ? "

" No ! "

" My dear Törless, if you rebel against us and don't put in an appearance, then you've got coming to you what came to Basini. You know the situation Reiting found you in. That's sufficient. Whether we have done more, or less, won't be of much help to you. We shall use everything against you. You're much too stupid and clumsy in such things to be a match for us.

"So if you don't see reason in good time, we shall expose you to the class as Basini's accomplice. Then it'll be up to him to protect you. Understand?"

A flood of threats, now from Beineberg, now from Reiting, and now uttered by both together, broke over Törless like a storm. And when they had both gone, he rubbed his eyes as if awakening from a dream. But of course it was just like Reiting really; in his anger he was capable of the utmost infamy, and Törless's offensive and mutinous words seemed to have cut him to the quick. And Beineberg? He had looked as if he were shaking with a hatred that he had been concealing for years—and this merely because he had made a fool of himself in front of Törless.

But the more menacingly events hung over Törless's head, the more indifferent he became and the more mechanical it all seemed to him. Their threats frightened him. So much he admitted to himself; but that was all. This danger had drawn him right into the maelstrom of reality.

He went to bed. He saw Beineberg and Reiting leave the dormitory, and then Basini shuffling wearily after them. But he did not follow.

Yet he was tortured by frightful imaginings. For the first time he thought of his parents again with some affection. He could feel that he needed the calm, safe ground of home if he was to consolidate and develop the things in himself that had hitherto only got him into trouble.

But what were these things? He had no time to think about it now and brood over what was going on. All he felt was an impassioned longing to escape from this confused, whirling state of things, a longing for quietness, for books. He felt his soul as black earth in which the seeds were already beginning to sprout, though nobody could yet know what flowers they would bear. He found himself thinking of a gardener, who waters his flower-beds at the break of every day, tending his plants with even, patient kindness. He could not rid himself of the image : that patient certainty seemed now to be the focus of all his longing. This was how it must be ! This was the way ! Törless now felt it clearly ; and, overruling all his fear and all his qualms, there was the conviction in him that he must exert himself to the utmost in order to attain that state of being.

The only thing he was not yet clear about was what had to be done next. For above all else this yearning for tranquil contemplativeness only heightened his loathing for the intrigues he was faced with now. Besides, he was really afraid of the vengeance that he had now to reckon with. If the other two really did set about defaming him to the class, trying to combat that would cost him a tremendous amount of energy ; and energy was the very thing he needed for other purposes just now. And the mere thought of this tangle of events, this collision with the intentions and the will-power of others, a collision so utterly lacking in any higher value, made him shudder with disgust.

And then he remembered a letter he had received from home quite a long time before. It was the answer to one he had written to his parents, telling them, as well as he could, about his peculiar states of mind, though this was before he had been drawn into the sexual adventure. Once again it was a thoroughly prosaic answer, full of well-meant, worthy, boring moral reflections, and it contained the advice to get Basini to give himself up and thus put an end to the undignified and dangerous state of subservience he was in.

Later on Törless had read this letter again when Basini

was lying naked beside him on the soft blankets in the lair. And it had given him special pleasure to savour these stolid, plain, sober words while reflecting that his parents, living as they did in that excessive brightness of everyday reality, were doubtless blind to the darkness in which his soul was now crouching, like some lithe and cat-like beast of prey.

But today it was with quite different feelings that he remembered that passage.

He felt himself being enfolded by a pleasant sense of relief, as though under the touch of a firm, kindly hand. In this moment the decision was made. A thought had flashed upon him, and he seized hold of it without a qualm, as though under the guidance of his parents.

He lay awake until the three came back. Then he waited until he could tell, by the regularity of their breathing, that they were asleep. Now he hastily tore a page out of his note-book and, by the dim flicker of the night-light, he wrote in large, wavering letters :

" They're going to hand you over to the class to-morrow. You're in for something terrible. The only way out is to go straight to the Head and confess. He would get to hear about it all anyway, only you'd be beaten half to death first.

" Put it all on R. and B. Say nothing about me.

" You can see I'm trying to save you."

He pushed this piece of paper into the sleeper's hand. Then, exhausted with excitement, he fell asleep too.

BEINEBERG and Reiting seemed willing to grant Törless respite for at least the whole of the next day.

But where Basini was concerned, things really got moving.

Törless saw Beineberg and Reiting going up to this boy and that, and watched groups forming round them, and eager whisperings going on.

And still he did not know whether Basini had found his note or not, for he had no chance to speak to him, feeling as he did that he was himself under observation.

As a matter of fact, at first he had been afraid they were talking about him too. But by now, when he was actually confronted with the danger, he was so paralysed by its repulsiveness that he could not have brought himself to lift a finger to ward it off.

It was only later that he joined one of the groups, hesitantly and quite expecting that they would all instantly turn against him.

But nobody took any notice of him. For the present it was only Basini against whom the hunt was up.

The excitement grew. Törless could see it growing. Reiting and Beineberg had doubtless added various lies of their own to the whole story.

At first there were grins on all faces, then some grew serious, and here and there hostile glances were cast in Basini's direction. Finally the class-room grew dense with a silence that was charged with tension, with dark, hot, sinister urges.

It happened to be a free afternoon.

They all gathered at the back of the room, by the lockers. Then Basini was summoned.

Beineberg and Reiting took up positions one on each side of him, like warders.

The doors having been locked and sentries posted, the customary procedure of stripping was carried out, to the general amusement.

Reiting had in his hand a packet of letters from Basini's mother to her son, and he began to read aloud.

" My dear little lad . . ."

There was a general guffaw.

" As you know, with the meagre financial resources that I, as a widow, have at my disposal . . ."

Ribald laughter and lewd jokes burst from the crowd. Reiting was about to continue his reading, when suddenly somebody gave Basini a push. Another boy, against whom he stumbled, pushed him away again, half jokingly and half in indignation. A third pushed him on a little further. And suddenly Basini, naked as he was, his mouth agape with terror, was being bounced around the room like a ball, to the accompaniment of laughter, cat-calls, and blows—now to this side of the room, now to that—getting bruised and cut on the sharp corners of desks, falling on to his knees, which were beginning to bleed ; and finally, streaked with blood and dust, with wildly staring, stupefied, glassy eyes, he collapsed on the floor and lay still, whereupon silence fell and everyone pressed forward to have a good look at him.

Törless shuddered. Now he had seen the terrible reality behind the threat Beineberg and Reiting had made.

And even now he still did not know what Basini was going to do.

Tomorrow night, it was resolved, Basini was to be tied to a bed and whipped with foils.

* * *

But to everyone's disconcerted surprise the head-master came into the classroom early in the morning. He was accompanied by the form-master and two other members of the staff. Basini was removed from the class and taken to a separate room.

Meanwhile the headmaster delivered an angry speech on the subject of the brutal bullying that had come to light and announced that there was going to be a very strict investigation into the matter.

Basini had given himself up.

Someone must have warned him of what was still in store for him.

NOBODY had any suspicions of Törless. He sat there quietly, sunk in his own thoughts, as though the whole thing did not concern him in the least.

Not even Reiting and Beineberg entertained the idea that he might be the traitor. They themselves had not taken their threats against him seriously; they had uttered them merely in order to intimidate him, in order to make him feel their superiority, and to some extent merely in the heat of the moment. Now, when their rage had passed off, they scarcely gave it another thought. What would in any case have prevented their treating Törless in a similar way was the fact of their being acquainted with his parents and having enjoyed their hospitality. This was so much a matter of course that it also prevented them from fearing any hostile act on his part.

Törless felt no remorse for what he had done. The furtive, cowardly quality about it did not count in comparison with the sense of complete liberation he now had. After all the agitation he had been through he now felt that everything within him was wonderfully clear and spacious.

He did not join in the excited conversations all round him about what was going to happen. He went quietly through the day's routine, keeping to himself.

When evening came and the lamps were lit, he sat down in his place, in front of him the copy-book in which he had made those hasty notes some time ago.

But he did not read them for long.   He smoothed the pages with his hand, and it seemed to him that there was a faint fragrance rising from them, like the scent of lavender that clings to old letters.   He was overcome by that tenderness mingled with melancholy which we always feel about a part of our life that irrevocably belongs to the past, when a delicate, pale shadow rises up out of that realm as though with withered flowers in its hands, and in its features we discover a forgotten likeness to ourselves.

And this mournful, faint shadow, this wan fragrance, seemed to be dissolving in a broad, full, warm stream— in life itself, which now lay open before him.

One phase of development was at an end; the soul had formed another annual ring, as a young tree does. And this feeling, as yet wordless, but overwhelming, in itself made up for all that had happened.

Now Törless began leafing through his old notes. The sentences in which he had clumsily recorded what was going on—that manifold amazement and bewilderment in the encounter with life—grew vivid again, and seemed to stir, and began to form a picture.   It all lay before him like a brightly lit path on which he could see the imprints of his own hesitant footsteps.   But something still seemed to be missing.   It was not a new idea that he needed.   Yet somehow the whole thing would not quite come to life for him.

He still felt unsure of himself.   And now there came the fear of having to stand in front of his teachers the next day and justify himself.   And how was he to do it?   How could he explain to them?   How could he make them understand that dark, mysterious way which he had gone?   Supposing they asked him why he had maltreated Basini, surely he could not answer: 'Because I was interested in something going on in my own mind, something I don't know much about even now, in spite of everything—something that makes all that I think about the whole thing seem quite unimportant.'

It was only a small matter, a single step between him and the termination of this phase in his mental development, but it appalled him, as though it were a monstrous abyss that lay ahead.

And even before nightfall Törless was in a state of feverish, panic-stricken excitement.

THE next day, when the boys were called up one by one for questioning, Törless was not to be found.

He had been last seen in the evening, sitting over a copy-book, apparently reading.

He was searched for throughout the building. Beineberg slipped away up to the lair to make sure that he was not there.

Finally it became evident that he had run away from school, and the police of the whole district were called upon to look out for him and asked to handle him, if he was found, with all possible discretion.

Meanwhile the enquiry began.

Reiting and Beineberg, who believed that Törless had run away out of fear of their threat of implicating him, felt themselves under an obligation to avert all suspicion from him, and they said everything they could in his favour.

They shifted all the blame on to Basini, and one by one the whole class bore witness to the fact that Basini was a thieving, low character who had responded to the most well-meaning attempts at reforming him only by repeating his offences again and again. Reiting solemnly declared that they realised they had acted wrongly, but that it had only been done because they were sorry for Basini and felt that one of their number should not be delivered up to punishment before every means of benevolent guidance had been tried. And once again the whole form asseverated that the ill-treatment of

Basini had been nothing but a spontaneous outbreak, since Basini had rewarded the noble sentiments of those who felt mercifully towards him with the most outrageous and vile derision.

In short, it was a well-rehearsed farce, brilliantly stage-managed by Reiting, and the highest possible moral tone was assumed in putting forward excuses that would find favour in the masters' eyes.

Basini preserved a stupefied silence, no matter what was said. He was still paralysed with terror from his experiences of two days earlier, and the solitary confinement in which he was kept, together with the quiet and matter-of-fact course of the investigation, was in itself a tremendous relief to him. All he wished for was that it might be over soon. Besides, Reiting and Beineberg had not failed to threaten him with the most atrocious revenge if he should dare to say anything against them.

Then Törless was brought in. He had been picked up, dead tired and very hungry, in the next town.

His flight now seemed to be the only mysterious element in the whole affair. But the situation was in his favour. Beineberg and Reiting had done their work well, talking about the nervy state he had been in recently and about his moral sensitiveness, which made him feel it was positively a crime that he, who had known about the whole matter all along, had not immediately gone and reported it, and by this omission had become partly responsible for the catastrophe.

As a result there was now a certain measure of sentimental benevolence in the masters' attitude to Törless, and his class-mates did not fail to prepare him for this.

Nevertheless, he was dreadfully agitated, and the fear of not being able to make himself intelligible almost exhausted him.

For reasons of discretion, since there was still a certain anxiety about possible revelations, the enquiry was being conducted in the headmaster's lodgings. Apart from the headmaster himself, those present were the form-master, the chaplain, and the mathematics master, to whom, as the youngest member of the staff, it fell to keep the minutes.

When Törless was asked why he had run away, he remained silent.

There was a general sympathetic wagging of heads.

"Well yes," the headmaster said, "I think we know all that is necessary about that. But now tell us what induced you to conceal Basini's offence."

It would have been easy for Törless to produce some lies now. But his nervousness had passed off and he was in fact tempted to talk about himself and to try out his ideas on them.

"I don't know exactly, sir. When I heard about it for the first time, it struck me as something quite mon-strous—simply unimaginable."

The chaplain looked complacent and gave Törless an encouraging nod.

"I—I couldn't help thinking about Basini's soul. . . ."

The chaplain beamed. The mathematics master polished his spectacles, replaced them, and narrowed his eyes. . . .

"I couldn't imagine what the moment must have been like when such a humiliation descended upon Basini, and this was what kept driving me to seek his company."

"Well, yes—in other words, you mean to say that you had a natural abhorrence of the particular error of your class-mate's ways, and that the sight of vice held you as it were spellbound, just as the gaze of the serpent is said to hold its victims."

The form-master and the mathematics master hastened

to express their appreciation of the simile by means of lively gestures.

But Törless said: "No, it wasn't actually abhorrence. It was like this: sometimes I told myself he had done wrong and ought to be reported to those in authority. . . ."

"And that is the way you should have acted."

"But then at other times he struck me as so peculiar that I simply didn't think about his being punished, I looked at him from quite a different point of view. It always gave me a jolt when I thought of him in that way. . . ."

"You must express yourself a little more clearly, my dear Törless."

"There isn't any other way of saying it, sir."

"Oh yes, there is, there is. You are excited. We can see that. You are perplexed and confused. What you said just now was very obscure."

"Well yes, I do feel perplexed. I have had much better ways of putting it. But it all comes to the same thing in the end—there was something quite weird in me. . . ."

"H'm, yes. But after all that is only natural in a matter like this."

Törless reflected for a moment.

"Perhaps one can put it like this: there are certain things that are destined to affect our lives in, as it were, two different ways. In my case they have been people, events, dark dusty corners, a high, cold, silent wall that suddenly came alive . . ."

"Good gracious, Törless, what is all this rambling talk?"

But Törless had suddenly begun to enjoy talking and getting it all off his chest.

". . . imaginary numbers . . ."

They all glanced now at one another, now at Törless. The mathematics master cleared his throat and said:

"I should like to interpolate, for the elucidation of these obscure allusions, that Törless here one day came to see me, asking for an explanation of certain fundamental mathematical concepts—with particular reference to that of imaginary numbers—things that are in fact very likely to be a cause of difficulty to the as yet insufficiently instructed intellect. I must indeed confess that he unquestionably displayed acuity of mind. On the other hand, he showed a really morbid insistence on singling out the very things which, so to speak, seemed —at least to him—to indicate a lacuna in the causality of thought.

"Do you remember what you said on that occasion, Törless?"

"Yes. I said it seemed to me that at these points we couldn't get across merely by the aid of thought, and we needed another and more inward sort of certainty to get us to the other side, as you might say. We can't manage solely by means of thinking, I felt that in the case of Basini too."

The headmaster was becoming impatient with this philosophical deviation from the direct line of the enquiry. But the chaplain was very satisfied with Törless's answer.

"So what you feel is that you are drawn away from science towards the religious aspect of things?" he asked, and then, turning to the others, went on: "Clearly it was really similar where Basini was concerned. The boy seems to have a receptive sensibility for the finer aspects, or as I should rather say, for the divine essence of morality that transcends the limits of our intellect."

Now the headmaster felt he was really obliged to take up the point.

" Well now, tell me, Törless, is it as the Reverend
Father says ? Have you an inclination to look behind
events or things—as you yourself have put it, in a rather
general way—seeking the religious background ? "

He himself would have been heartily glad if Törless
had at long last given an affirmative answer and thus
provided a solid basis on which to judge his case.

But Törless said : " No, it wasn't that either."

" Well, then for heaven's sake, boy, will you please
tell us plainly *what* it was ! " the headmaster burst out.
" After all, we cannot possibly settle down to a philosophical discussion with you ! "

But now Törless became stubborn. He himself felt
that he had not put his case well, but both the antagonism
and the misguided approval he had met with gave him
a sense of haughty superiority over these older men who
seemed to know so little about the inner life of a human
being.

" I can't help its not being all these things you meant.
But I myself can't explain properly what I felt each time.
Still, if I say what I think about it now, you may understand why it took me so long to tear myself away from
it."

He was standing very straight, as proudly as if he were
the judge here ; and he looked straight ahead, past the
men facing him—he could not bear the sight of this
ridiculous assembly.

There outside the window was a crow, perching on a
branch. Apart from that there was nothing but the vast
white plain.

He felt that the moment had come when he would talk
clearly, coherently, and triumphantly of the things that
had at first been vague and tormenting within him, and
later had been lifeless, without force.

It was not that any new idea had come to him, lending

him this confidence and lucidity. He simply felt it throughout his being, as he stood there drawn up to his full height and as though standing in the middle of an empty room—felt it with the whole of his being, just like that time when he had let his astonished gaze stray over his class-mates as they sat there writing or memorising, all busily at work.

For it is strange how it is with thoughts. They are often no more than accidentals that fade out again without leaving any trace ; and thoughts have their dead and their vital seasons. We sometimes have a flash of understanding that amounts to the insight of genius, and yet it slowly withers, even in our hands—like a flower. The form remains, but the colours and the fragrance are gone. That is to say, we still remember it all, word for word, and the logical value of the proposition, the discovery, remains entirely unimpaired, and nevertheless it merely drifts aimlessly about on the surface of our mind, and we do not feel ourselves any the richer for it. And then, perhaps years later—all at once there is again a moment when we see that in the meantime we have known nothing of it, although in terms of logic we have known it all.

Yes, there are dead and living thoughts. The process of thinking that takes place on the illumined surface, and which can always be checked and tested by means of the thread of causality, is not necessarily the living one. A thought that one encounters in this way remains as much a matter of indifference as any given man in a column of marching soldiers. Although a thought may have entered our brain a long time earlier, it comes to life only in the moment when something that is no longer thought, something that is not merely logical, combines with it and makes us feel its truth beyond the realm of all justification, as though it had dropped an anchor that tore into the blood-warm, living flesh. . . . Any great flash of understanding is only half completed in the illumined circle of the conscious mind ; the other half takes place in the dark loam of our innermost being. It is primarily a state of soul, and uppermost, as it were at the extreme tip of it, there the thought is—poised like a flower.

Törless had needed only one great shock to his soul at this time to bring this out in him at last, flowering in the light.

Without paying any attention to the disconcerted faces round about him, and as though soliloquising, he started out from this point and spoke right on without a pause, his eyes fixed on some far distance.

" Perhaps I don't know enough yet to find the right words for it, but I think I can describe it. It happened again just a moment ago. I don't know how to put it except by saying that I see things in two different ways— everything, ideas included. If I make an effort to find any difference in them, each of them is the same today as it was yesterday, but as soon as I shut my eyes they're suddenly transformed, in a different light. Perhaps I went wrong about the imaginary numbers. If I get to them by going straight along inside mathematics, so to speak, they seem quite natural. It's only if I look at them directly, in all their strangeness, that they seem impossible. But of course I may be all wrong about this, I know too little about it. But I wasn't wrong about Basini. I wasn't wrong when I couldn't turn my ear away from the faint trickling sound in the high wall or my eye from the silent, swirling dust going up in the beam of light from a lamp. No, I wasn't wrong when I talked about things having a second, secret life that nobody takes any notice of ! I—I don't mean it literally —it's not that things are alive, it's not that Basini seemed to have two faces—it was more as if I had a sort of second sight and saw all this not with the eyes of reason. Just as I can feel an idea coming to life in my mind, in the same way I feel something alive in me when I look at things and stop thinking. There's something dark in me, deep under all my thoughts, something I can't measure out with thoughts, a sort of life that can't be expressed in words and which is my life, all the same. . . .

" That silent life oppressed me, harrassed me. Something kept on making me stare at it. I was tormented by the fear that our whole life might be like that and that I was only finding it out here and there, in bits and pieces. . . . Oh, I was dreadfully afraid ! I was out of my mind. . . ."

These words and these figures of speech, which were far beyond what was appropriate to Törless's age, flowed easily and naturally from his lips in this state of vast excitement he was in, in this moment of almost poetic inspiration. Then he lowered his voice and, as though moved by his own suffering, he added :

" Now it's all over. I know now I was wrong after all. I'm not afraid of anything any more. I know that things are just things and will probably always be so. And I shall probably go on for ever seeing them sometimes this way and sometimes that, sometimes with the eyes of reason, and sometimes with those other eyes. . . . And I shan't ever try again to compare one with the other. . . ."

He fell silent. He took it quite as a matter of course that now he could go, and nobody tried to stop him.

* * *

When he had left the room, the masters looked at each other with baffled expressions.

The headmaster wagged his head irresolutely. It was the form-master who first found something to say.

"Dear me, it strikes me that this little prophet was trying to give us a lecture! It's the very dickens to know what to make of him! Such excitement! And at the same time this bewilderment, this perplexity, about quite simple things!"

"Receptivity and spontaneity of mind," the mathematics master concurred. "Apparently he has been attaching too much importance to the subjective factor in all our experience, and this is what perplexed him and drove him to use those obscure metaphors."

Only the chaplain was silent. In all Törless's talk it was the often recurring word 'soul' that had caught his attention, and he would gladly have taken the boy under his wing.

But then, again, he was not entirely sure what had been meant by it.

However, the headmaster put an end to the situation. "I do not know what is really going on in this boy Törless, but there is no doubt about it that he is in such an extreme state of nervous tension that boarding-school is in all probability no longer what is most suitable for him. What he needs is a more thorough supervision of his intellectual diet than we are in a position to provide. I do not think that we can continue to bear the responsibility. Törless ought to be educated privately. I shall write to his father along these lines."

All hastened to agree to this excellent suggestion on the part of the worthy headmaster.

"He was really so odd that I could almost believe he has some predisposition to hysteria," the mathematics master said to the colleague at his side.

*   *   *

At the same time that Törless's parents received the

213

headmaster's letter they also received one from Törless himself, in which he asked them to take him away from the school, since he no longer felt it was the right place for him.

MEANWHILE Basini had been expelled, and things at school had resumed their normal course.

It had been decided that Törless was to be fetched away by his mother. It was with indifference that he said good-bye to his class-mates. He was almost beginning to forget their names already.

He had never again gone up to the little red room. All that seemed to lie far, far behind him.

Since Basini's expulsion it all seemed dead. It was almost as if that boy, in whom all those relationships had intertwined, had broken the circuit with his departure.

A sort of quietness and scepticism had come over Törless ; his desperation had gone. 'I suppose it was just those furtive goings-on with Basini that made everything seem so frantic,' he thought to himself. Otherwise there did not seem to be anything to account for it.

But he was ashamed—just as one is ashamed in the morning after a feverish night during which, from all the corners of the dark room, one has seen dreadful threats looming up and about to overwhelm one.

His behaviour at the interview in the headmaster's room now struck him as unspeakably ridiculous. What a fuss ! Hadn't they been quite right ? Such a fuss about a little thing like that ! But still, there was something in him that robbed this humiliation of its sting. 'I suppose I did behave unreasonably,' he reflected. 'All the same, the whole thing seems altogether to have had very little to do with my reason.' For this was his new feeling about it. He had the memory of a tremendous storm that had raged within him, but all he could muster by way of explanation for it now was entirely inadequate. 'So I suppose it must have been something much more fundamental and inevitable,' he concluded, 'than anything that can be dealt with by means of reasoned argument. . . .'

And the thing that had been there even before passion seized him, the thing that had only been overgrown by that passion—the real thing, the problem itself—was still firmly lodged in him. It was this mental perspective that he had experienced, which alternated according to whether he was considering what was distant or what was near by; it was this incomprehensible relationship that according to our shifts of standpoint gives happenings and objects sudden values that are quite incommensurable with each other, strange to each other. . . .

All this, and the rest besides, he saw remarkably clear and pure—and small. It was as one sees things in the morning, when the first pure rays of sunlight have dried the sweat of terror, when table and cupboard, enemy and fate, all shrink again, once more assuming their natural dimensions.

But just as then there remains a faint, brooding lassitude, so too it was with Törless. He now knew how to distinguish between day and night; actually he had always known it, and it was only that a monstrous dream had flowed like a tide over those frontiers, blotting them out. He was ashamed of the perplexity he had been in. But still there was also the memory that it could be otherwise, that there were fine and easily effaced boundary-lines around each human being, that feverish dreams prowled around the soul, gnawing at the solid walls and tearing open weird alleys—and this memory had sunk deep into him, sending out its wan and shadowy beams.

He could not quite have explained this. But his inability to find words for it, this near-dumbness, was in itself delightful, like the certainty of a teeming body that can already feel in all its veins the faint tugging of new life. Confidence and weariness intermingled in Törless. . . .

So it was that he waited quietly and meditatively for the moment of departure.

His mother, who had expected to find an overwrought and desperately perplexed boy, was struck by his cool composure.

When they drove out to the railway station, they passed, on the right, the little wood with the house in it where Božena lived. It looked utterly insignificant and harmless, merely a dusty thicket of willow and alder.

And Törless remembered how impossible it had been for him then to imagine the life his parents led. He shot a sidelong glance at his mother.

" What is it, my dear boy ? "

" Nothing, Mamma. I was just thinking."

And, drawing a deep breath, he considered the faint whiff of scent that rose from his mother's corseted waist.

PANTHEON MODERN CLASSICS

MEMED, MY HAWK
by Yashar Kemal

The most important novel to come out of modern Turkey, this vital and exciting story of a latter-day Robin Hood is set against the beauty and brutality of Turkish peasant life. "Exciting, rushing, lyrical, a complete and subtle emotional experience."—*Chicago Sun-Times*

0-394-71016-9 $6.95

THE LEOPARD
by Giuseppe di Lampedusa

This powerful novel of a Sicilian prince perched on the brink of great historic change is widely acknowledged as a masterpiece of European literature. "The finest historical novel I have read in years."—*Saturday Review*

0-394-74949-9 $5.95

YOUNG TÖRLESS
by Robert Musil

Taut, compelling, pitiless first novel by the author of *The Man Without Qualities*. A meticulous account, set in an Austrian military academy, of the discovery and abuse of power—physical, emotional, and sexual. "An illumination of the dark places of the heart everywhere."—*Washington Post*

0-394-71015-0 $5.95

THE STORY OF A LIFE
by Konstantin Paustovsky

Universally acclaimed memoir of Russian boyhood coming of age amidst war and revolution. A startlingly vivid, deeply personal yet panoramic view of Russia during the tumultuous first two decades of the twentieth century. "A work of astonishing beauty . . . a masterpiece."—Isaac Bashevis Singer

0-394-71014-2 $8.95